JesusDevil
The Parables

Praise for *JesusDevil*:

"In this timely work, Alexis weaves through and beyond the many ways that a parable can live. She speaks of viruses, sheltering in and folks losing their sense of taste in stories where the dead rise, slay, shake themselves loose and rumble us with their sexy. In this afiction, ancient beings from the future take us down and up roads that can only be detailed in a structure that defies naming. Once again, Alexis has written a book of holy queer, new possibilities. Get ready to open, pause, and wonder."
— **Sharon Bridgforth**, author of Lambda Literary Finalist *love conjure/blues*

"Our ancestral past, present, and future share a concentric relationship in De Veaux's prophetic, *JesusDevil: The Parables*. In these after (other) worlds, Black life is autopoietic. Black life recreates, reproduces, and changes shape, sound, and color. *JesusDevil* arranges and makes meaning and rhythm through erotic exercise and language. These articulations of the sacred are not about orthodox practice; they are 'black sermonic text' of the quotidian, an aesthetic of the ordinary. The body, as De Veaux poeticizes, expands language and biology. The body *pussys* both itself and other, the body is self and other. De Veaux's nine parables are vestibules of possibility and proof that the imagination is the genesis of promise." —**Briona Simone Jones**, editor of Lambda Literary Award winner *Mouths of Rain: An Anthology of Black Lesbian Thought*

"In this utterly authentic, deftly crafted, and creatively courageous book, Alexis De Veaux illustrates how the apex of form, style, and matter are more than the tools to document and journey through individual and collective memory; rather, this trinity of craft must, can, has been, and will be reimagined in the ritual of storytelling as a portal of constant creation, not simply a tale told simply to arrive someplace and settle. When Fhill, De Veaux's central character, says she wants 'a big life-changing prize or honor that recognizes all we been through over time,' I thought immediately that *JesusDevil: The Parables* is that prize. It generously invites readers into a dogged literacy, a rigorous reading practice so that we might be fully awash in the complexity of life in spirit, and spirit in life, presented in all its honesty, love, humor, desire, pleasure, pain, and grace. *JesusDevil: The Parables* is the fulcrum upon which ancestral listening as a technology of writing otherwise, manifests as both possibility and practice. It is a gift to have this book in this time, and now, for all times." —**Eric Darnell Pritchard**, author of *Fashioning Lives: Black Queers and the Politics of Literacy*

JesusDevil,
The Parables

Alexis De Veaux

Foreword by
adrienne maree brown

EMERGENT STRATEGY SERIES

Emergent Strategy by adrienne maree brown
Pleasure Activism by adrienne maree brown
Undrowned by Alexis Pauline Gumbs
We Will Not Cancel Us by adrienne maree brown
Holding Change by adrienne maree brown
Begin the World Over by Kung Li Sun
Fables and Spells by adrienne maree brown
Liberated to the Bone by Susan Raffo

JesusDevil: The Parables
Emergent Strategy Series No. 8
© 2023 Alexis De Veaux

This edition © 2023, AK Press

ISBN: 978-1-84935-506-3
E-ISBN: 978-1-84935-507-0
Library of Congress Control Number: 9781849355063

AK Press   AK Press
370 Ryan Avenue #100   33 Tower St.
Chico, CA 95973   Edinburgh EH6 7BN
USA   Scotland
www.akpress.org   www.akuk.com
akpress@akpress.org   akuk@akpress.org

Please contact us to request the latest AK Press distribution catalog, which features books, pam-
phlets, zines, and stylish apparel published and/or distributed by AK Press. Alternatively, visit
our websites for the complete catalog, latest news, and secure ordering.

Cover design by Herb Thornby
Printed in the United States of America on acid-free paper

Ruby Moore Hill
(1898–1989)

My grandmother
Who, in her afterlife, came in a dream to tell me
She—who as a child picked fields in North Carolina
And was forced to work as a maid in
New York City when she migrated north
Earned $364 for the year 1939—
She came to me in a dream
She said, "I am a femme now"

Foreword

by adrienne maree brown

Alexis De Veaux is wholly unique and prone to stunning the breath out of my system. I knew this before we ever met, reading her text *Yabo*. I knew this watching her enter a room where Jewelle Gomez was offering a brilliant interpretation of James Baldwin on the stage in front of us, and yet Alexis, at the front of the audience, was the force of gravity for the room's attention. I knew this the first time I entered her home, which feels like the spirit of Mardi Gras and Alice in Wonderland and Mickalene Thomas co-created the best ritual library of all time. I know this every time I find myself in conversation with Alexis, that she wants the highest quality breath I can offer, the deepest-rooted thinking any of us can offer.

In the summer of 2020, I was watching a plenary from the Allied Media Conference, broadcast on my parents' TV. COVID-19 revealed to me that I hadn't spent enough time with my parents, so I went to them, quarantined, and stayed for four months. I learned that I would never get enough time with them as long as I live but that I could make the time we had together more sacred, more present. Alexis helped me see that.

The panel was called *Writing the Future,* and it featured Alexis De Veaux in conversation with my beloved comrades and collaborators Alexis Pauline Gumbs and Walidah Imarisha.

I wrote down the things Alexis De Veaux was saying, because they felt like instruction and permission:

"I have to create first and live inside of that. I have to not judge what comes through."

"I am not just writing against whiteness, homophobia, ableism ... but with every project I am asking myself what am I writing towards? Am I creating Black shamanic texts? Is it sonic, heard, vibrational, disturbing the air?"

And then she said that what she was currently writing was called *afiction*, something that was coming through her that was not built as a linear story of generated characters but as a revealed poetics of gathered and ever-changing spirit. I knew what she meant in my bones, and I needed it—I asked if I could help get it into the world through our small and mighty series at AK Press.

With the Emergent Strategy Series, we are interested in provocation, in offering up new lenses, frameworks, and forms through which humans can see where we are and what we need to attend to; stories that tell the truth, theories that can be practiced in current time. We need new genre and post-genre work that blurs the line of collaboration with spirit.

Alexis was generous with us, and if I'm honest I thought perhaps she was just indulging me as an eager fan-reader. As she sent me the *JesusDevil* parables she had written to that point, I read them immediately and asked for more. I felt like I had won a literary lottery for my soul. What I got to read, what you are about to read, is a text that I believe will take its place in Black feminist classic creative literature alongside Toni Cade Bambara's *The Salt Eaters*, Ntozake Shange's *For Colored Girls Who Have Considered Suicide ... When the Rainbow is Enuf*, with the spirit mystery of Toni Morrison's *Beloved*. And—it is unlike any of these, or anything else I've ever read.

Reader, this text is to be felt as much as read. You will have to trust your intuition and release your assumptions. The character-spirits will slip off the page and into the world around you, seduce you, shock you, open you up, change you—and you will miss them after, trust me. The poetic form of this storytelling will guide you through transgression, wonderment, and pleasure, but the destination will in part be your own.

I am beyond honored that Alexis De Veaux trusted Emergent Strategy with this sky-shaking work. Turn the page and give her your breath.

Preface
TO PARABLE

verb

To evade the capture, servitude, or imprisonment of one's erotic(s);

To inhabit a black otherwhere, as do (other) "loci of aesthetics" such as song, dance, language, visual and body arts
(see Dr. Salah Hassan, University at Buffalo, Department of History of Art, graduate course class notes, circa 1992);

To live in states of being not yet in existence;
To suture, or disembogue;
To display or experience a violent beauty, an insistence on violent forms of beauty, the beautification of enslaved blackness;

To live in a reality different from other or known realities;

To have one's interiority supersede, erase, such that systems of domination cannot flourish in "the black interior" (see Elizabeth Alexander, *The Black Interior: Essays,* 2004);

To avenge historical suffering;

To tell oneself an erogenous story while engaging in acts of self pleasure and pleasing the self, as in "What were you doing up there (in your room), pussying yourself?"

To arrive within the choreography of ancestral desire(s), as in not who is queer but what is queer, as in the desire of life and afterlife to promote, articulate, and further difference;

To become a triangle, as in the spoken the unspoken the unspeakable all at once i.e., the historical black she—those individuals, irrespective of gender, who identified as, identified with, assumed, and wore the mantle of black and female in the so-called "new world whose feet carry my feet, whose breath I breathe;

To create a black sermonic text as structure, as guide, beyond externalizing sites of religion and religious documents and edifice, such that the secular realms of the everyday, articulate the sacred

(An) Other Realm

I call these parables *afiction*. Afiction moves away from, beyond, fiction; taking with it some of the tropes of fiction (story, plot) and leaving others behind (characters, overdependence on exposition, for example). It furthers a poetics of repair, doing, love, desire, and freedom as body parts of blackness. Afiction recognizes what the queer Kenyan intellectual Keguro Macharia calls "political vernaculars," words and phrases that draw us into political discussion, foreground the political, and "create possibilities for different ways of coming together."[1] As Macharia theorizes, "freedom and love are powerful vernaculars."[2] Inherent to freedom and love are opportunities for a vernacular that is "untethered to state imaginaries."[3] In other words, we can speak a language that constructs the difference between being legally "freed" by the state, and imagining what black freedom looks, feels, smells, tastes like everyday.

Whereas the purpose of fiction is to describe imaginary events and people (characters), afiction attempts to write into and materialize, make material, existence of the spiritual. In this work, *JesusDevil, The Parables*, spirits populate the parables and live as animal, plant, human, and extrahuman forms. They live in an Afrosurrealist time envelope, "a future-past called RIGHT NOW" that is "necessary to transform how we see things now, how we look at what happened then, and what we can expect to see in the future."[4] As such, the writing relies on memory and rememory as constitutive of blackness in and across time and seeks to inhabit story rather than tell it. In afiction, I am writing into an other realm.

I believe I am always and already writing not just against but toward. I came to this belief some years ago, as I began to think about writing to center the possible rather than the what is. Antiblackness, homophobia, sexism and genderism, patriarchy, class hierarchies, capitalism and empire, white supremacy, ageism, and fear

---

1   Keguro Macharia, "Political Vernaculars: Freedom and Love," *The New Inquiry*, March 14, 2016, https://thenewinquiry.com/political-vernaculars-freedom-and-love.

2   Macharia, "Political Vernaculars: Freedom and Love."

3   Macharia, "Political Vernaculars: Freedom and Love."

4   D. Scot Miller. "Afrosurreal Manifesto: Black Is the New black—21st Century Manifesto," *Black Camera* 5, no. 1 (2013): 113–117.

of the abilities of differing, divergent bodies; these, and more, constitute the what is, the ways in which multiple kinds of human life are rendered unworthy, throw away, not human. Writing towards the possible allows me to think of black life, to speculate black life, as framed by adaptation, cultural transfer, mystery (that which defies western models of logic), and the dynamic of unstable realities. The possible, I have come to consider, is not utopia, nor is it dystopia.

Rather than addressing normative concerns of society organized around notions of either a perfect state or a post-apocalyptic one, the possible can be a platform for "black alter-world-making and refusal to participate in the perceived reality of dominant consensus, with its assumed parameters and priorities."[5] The possible is (an) other realm of meaning, an otherwhere, a "metaphysical space beyond" the stereotypes of "the black public everyday."[6] I have used my imagination to access it, but it is not imaginary.

This afiction is writing seeded in West Africa—where the majority of Africans who were enslaved originated. My people were brought to this place from West Africa. The trace of them in my DNA tells me they were from Nigeria, Cameroon, Congo, and Western Bantu; from Mali, Benin, and Togo; from the Ivory Coast and Ghana. Among other forms of cultural transfers, they brought with them what they could reconstruct of their masquerade traditions. How could they not? How could they not try to reenact what they knew, what was spiritual for them, what might sustain their survival in this brutal, alien world? I know now that their masquerade narratives, their stories, were lessons that framed an organic literary discourse as performance; were adapted to withstand the challenges my people faced in new environments in the Caribbean and the colonies; promoted a sense of identity, cause, or ideology; and helped them to recover or reshape their collective consciousness in an unstable, constantly changing world.[7] I see these twenty-first century parables as descendants, as models, though not exact replicas, of my ancestors' traditions; as a kind of cultural

---

5   Jayna Brown. *Black Utopias, Speculative Life and the Music of Other Worlds* (Durham: Duke University Press, 2021), 12.

6   Elizabeth Alexander, *The Black Interior, Essays* (Saint Paul: Graywolf Press, 2004), x.

7   Raphael Chijioke Njoku, *West African Masking Traditions and Diaspora Masquerade Carnivals, History, Memory, and Transnationalism* (Rochester, NY: University of Rochester Press, 2020), 2.

diffusion that is dynamic and does not need to recreate the original in order to be of the original.[8]

I wrote these parables as they came to me. I did not make outlines or make use of other literary technologies of writing. The one thing I was certain of was that there would be a spirit in human form named Fhill who would be the primary thread between the parables. The imprint of the next one or two parables always came as I was working with the one in front of me. Words, colors, names, and whole or fragments of sentences are repeated, in different contexts, across the parables. I hand wrote them in black-and-white composition books. And when I typed them all up finally, I typed them as I would poems; a nod to my grandmother who taught me to read the Bible, its parables, as poetry. Though I did not know it immediately, I soon realized the practice was less about writing than it was about listening; listening to and in an other realm. I was a receiver, and I came to witness writing as the practice of receiving. There were days when I received a single word, or just a few sentences, or a few pages, an idea, something to be inserted, a rewrite. And there were days of nothing, no matter how hard I thought I was listening. Some years ago, I complained about my writing going slow to the visual artist Valerie Maynard. A sculptor, Valerie's practice was to live with a newly acquired piece of wood or stone, to sit with it until the spirit inside the material revealed itself to her; only then did she pick up her tools and carve away until the spirit was revealed. She advised me, wisely, "It's all in the reveal, Alexis. You cannot write what hasn't been revealed." Revelation is the touch of the spirit. When I waited, I received.

---

8 Njoku, *West African Masking Traditions*, 1.

SYNOPSIS

JesusDevil: The Parables centers upon a black queer spirit who lives in human form. The spirit is known as Fhill. Fhill is the connective thread between a series of parables. Though referred to as "she," Fhill is neither typically female nor typically male and, as such, queers both as fluid rather than stable categories of identity. Fhill travels through nine experiences in life, nine parables, that examine aspects of being black and human—living with a nonhuman being; desire; memory; inherited black life; social constructions of blackness; revenge; sex; challenges to what we call health; black life itself. *JesusDevil, The Parables* is told as a nonlinear, deeply urban narrative that examines some of the ways city life arranges black spiritual expression.

The Parables

GIRL NEGRO

She was tired of living these black lives.
Hurting that hurt.
But what other kind of life was available to her if not the one in 1739
and the Stono Rebellion, South Carolina.
Why hadn't she come back as different.
What was the chance she could.
What was chance anyway, if not a galactic event.
Serial happenings.
Spontaneous combustion.
What the galaxy belches in its spit.
The eventful uneventful eruption of billions of years and how many encounters
with chance did the galaxy afford the syntax of a human life

Hurt of and in the body when she was 28 in the 2015
hanged in a jail cell in Texas.
What did chance deracinate in the body.
What disembogued from a life

In the body was the counterpublic: she.
In the 16th Street Baptist Church bombing
1963, Birmingham

Where was the sanctuary from.
The disparity: in pain even living in wealth.
And that was the archaeology of the hurt in Live Oak, Florida. When
she drove to the office of the Dr. Clifford Leroy Adams the white prominent.
Who'd sired her child Loretta.
That hurt.
Raped her, a well-to-do mother, for years.
So she entered through the Colored Entrance. The sanctuary from.
With her .38.

Shot the assumption of white men's paramour rights to black women's sex.
Shot that 1952, dead

In a year that was unrecorded.
She was an artifact.
An artifact in an archive of rampant, pollutant spread.
Of a cancer in the body politic she escaped from on foot.
Through, like other run-way, the insect and snake and black bear infested
Dismal Swamp between North Carolina and Virginia.
All the way to the free state Pennsylvania.
With the sickly woman she loved carried on her back.
Black lives and the centuries of.
Husolank[9]: captivity and forced labor and strange gods and fields and fucked
and starved and used for and shack houses and lynched and newspaper walls
and maid and raped dreams and shot down and lack and centuries, husolank
my descendants, centuries and
when it gon' stop

And now it was this 1948 life.
This Sex: Girl. Color or Race: Negro. On her birth certificate.
The prominent doctor's handwriting in the penmanship of the state.
No family story of named after or look like before her come back as.
She was a monstrosity.
Her mother's last name hers now but no given name for her.
Her father's information left blank.
He was invisible, or worse, nonexistent.
Girl Negro.
The stamp of an unworthy life

But she had the ancestors' kiss.
So what they dreamed she dreamed.
And she worked the dream.

---

9 Hoosolank [hoo-so-lank], *verb*: to help someone remember something from a previous or future
   life. Word created by Ella Engel-Snow, www.livingdictionaryproject.com/invented-words.

She sucked up an underground railroad of rupture, of rhizomatic black pain.
In these bodies that had been her life

It was a story of the body of the body.
It was a tale of thosmies[10]

So she made up this black.
Out of the technologies of her inheritance: black poor pussy.
Her black was a homemade aesthetic.
Shared with her dead uncle's shoeshine box.
His boyhood dream of wealth and freedom.
Painted black, like her. She cherished it.
And what held it together all these years: its body.
The cans of polish, the shine cloths, and the brushes
she identified with his dedication to beauty.
Present now more than ever

In her uncle's eye she saw her own muscle.
The refusal to accept a less-than life. That was beauty.
Beauty was there in the planet's imagination, those fresh roses
on her dining table always.
The means to come and go.
How she carried herself head up and eye to eye in public.
That was beauty.
Something good to eat week after week.
A dollar in her pocket and two in the bank. Rampant beauty.
She was alive alive.
But it was not just her life she was living.
She was living black remember.
And so she, and through her, we, thrived.
In spite of the palimpsest, the metastasis of the white.
Thrive. That was beauty.

---

10 Thosmies [hoss-me-zes], *verb*: 1. The act of eating the flesh of words; 2. The carnal knowl-
edge of the tongue. Word created by Alexis De Veaux, www.livingdictionaryproject.com/
invented-words.

The antidote to the cartographies, the chaos, of these lives.

The cumulative impact of them since 1619.

Compounded by brutalized, and time compounded by pain.

Because we were, by our persistent living, the provocation

Fhill was not a pessimist.

But neither could she invest anymore in the fuckery hope.

Hope had disabled black people.

Some, talked about black lives matter.

They did not, she knew now.

She'd lived enough of them, across enough time.

Black lives did not, never did, matter as life forms in this place.

Hope was a distraction.

And its opposite was printed on her favorite tee shirt

like a black sermonic text: *We Out. Harriet Tubman, 1849*

And still, in spite of all her efforts, it had come to this:

You're depressed, Orrl said. It was always something when her mother called. It was tiring being her mother's mother.

You really think that's it, Fhill said. Her breath rattled.

Yes, Mom, Orrl said. You've been spending too much time alone.

Fhill's heart raged in her chest, a wild, captured thing.

I don't think I'm depressed, she said. I don't think black people are depressed.

We *do get* depressed, Orrl countered.

Yes, I know, Fhill said. But that's what it looks like from the outside.

Though the outside and the inside were independent they also co-created each other.

Inside us, she thought, black people had known more than our share of human suffering.

Our suffering had enormity.

It had an expanse, an intensity so devastating we lived sicker and died younger.

Life frustrated, murdered, our possible.

And what we suffered was non-catastrophic:

Suffering did not strike us with the quick of the lightening bolt.

Our suffering *was* the lightening bolt.
Until death.
It felled our grandparents, our parents, and us.
In succession.[11] Across genders

So I don't think that's it, Fhill said to her daughter
Mom—Orrl put her foot down. Call up one of your friends. Go out on a date.
I gotta go—
Orrl ended the call hurriedly.
She snatched up her backpack and keys.
She couldn't deal with her mother's anxieties right now.
She was horny.
Overness, that delicious black confection, was waiting for her at The Fabulous.
The night was already tumescent

Fhill called Emma.
Sounds like you're having a panic attack, Emma said.
What? Fhill said.
An overwhelming fear, Emma said. A sense of imminent danger.
She peeked out the kitchen window.
Lune sat on the shed's roof with Leaf, their youngest. Still as
the figurine of the cat goddess, Bast, on her altar.
The father and daughter gazed at something on the ground Emma could not
see.
Fhill's gaze went inward.
It feels like a change is gonna come, she said.
O, hell yeah, Emma said, let's have some Sam Cooke conjuration up in here.
Then she crooned into her phone:

> *Its been a long time comin'*
> *But I know oh-oo-oh*
> *A change gon' come*

---

11 William R. Jones, "Theodicy and Racism," *A Troubling In My Soul, Womanist Perspectives on Evil and Suffering*, ed. Emilie M. Townes (Maryknoll, NY: Orbis Books, 1993), 22.

Oh yes it will

Sing it with me baby, Emma said. We had some good times on this one.
Sing it—

Its been too hard living

Fhill gave in and they sang to each other:

But I'm afraid to die
Cause I don't know what's up there
Beyond the sky

Fawn strolled into the kitchen headed for the refrigerator.
The teenager rolled her eyes at her mother and mimicked vomiting before she
went out again, a bottle of water in hand.
Emma laughed into the phone.
You'll be all right, *cher*, she said to Fhill. You need to *laissez les bon temps rouler*.
I need to get my due, Fhill said.
Your due?
Yeah, Emm. Whatum due. A big, life-changing prize. Or a honor. Something
that recognizes all we been through over time. *All* we been through.
Life ain't like that, Emma said.
And once again, Fhill peered inside herself.
She could see hurt filtering through her liver.
In her plasma and blood cells and platelets.
The remember. That keloided heart and bowels.
That let her shed and live with, simultaneously.
As it salted muscle to sinew.
But the brutal killing of an innocent black woman by police,
in her own home, that morning,
a no-knock invasion.
When was the cumulative weight of pain,
gon' stop

Life ain't one life, Fhill said to Emma.
I'll come over and cook for you, Emma said.
No thanks, Fhill said.
Why not, Emma said.
Fhill went silent.
And then, because her inside conspired to be heard,
she blurted out—
I don't even like being human.
And I'm tired of living like one.

Well, this outburst was no surprise to the ancestors listening in.
For some human time, an incalculable measure in the vernacular of
The Divine,
they'd been spectators to Fhill's stoic battles with the narrative black life.
They'd absorbed her, breathed with her, kept her going regardless.
Because life, they believed, desired life

Some of the ancestors though, the ones furthest from now,
cried in collective wonder.
If life desired life, didn't life also desire to survive.
But didn't death make being alive ever more urgent.
Without death there was no life.
Ahh, yes, offered the youngest.
But how much enmity can a life form tolerate

And now the ancestors began to argue.
Did it sound like she wanted to die.
Death was the ever-present possibility.
Perhaps Fhill thought she'd failed at being alive.
That was understandable, surely.
Aliveness had a right to fail.
If it was *to be* alive.
But didn't death urge life to be creative.
And didn't life's success include its suffering.
Yes, but.

She'd *never said* she *wanted* to die, an ancestor noted.

Well what *do* she want, they queried each other.

Until, after tossing that question about the abundant dark matter,

they all finally agreed:

Their descendant wanted to transition.

Not because she wanted to die.

Because she wanted to be differently alive.

And so when Fhill went to sleep that night, still troubled by

her conversations with Orrl and Emma,

the ancestors granted what they believed was Fhill's desire.

The human form was not necessary to life.

But what it was made of—carbon, hydrogen, nitrogen, oxygen, phosphorus, and

sulfur—what she was made of,

was

THE LORD OF GOOD PUSSY

Two days after moving into the neighborhood, Fhill ventured out.
At the other end of her new block and across the street, she spotted
the store's black glass door.
Thinking it entrance to one of those upscale coffee bars that'd sprouted
all over Harlem of late.
Fhill pushed open the glass door and walked into memory

The proprietor, The Lord, looked out unseen from the light-emitting wall.
In it, stars and planets, milky ways and galaxies constantly shifted
within the invisible glue, its dark matter,
that connected the neighborhoods of space.
The Lord watched Fhill's nosiness teeter about the neat chaos.
An odd collection of antique weather vanes, gauges, globes, clocks, telescopes,
and sundry knick-knacks piled atop each other
in glass showcases. On the floor. Leaning against the walls.
Was to Fhill just a humongous mess overwhelming the small space.
As the proprietor stepped out of the wall, Fhill stepped toward
the glass case that was the store's counter.
Gingerly

Can I help you?
The Lord's voice was a rich dirty bass that, uncomfortable having been trotted
out this early, Fhill felt the thunderclap of in her own chest.
She stared at the cumulus mass of indigo afro encircling the delicate, flawlessly
made-up face.
And that skin.
Was shades of black painted on top of black.
Black came through the light of the black before the black
Fhill was looking at.
Galactic black

I'm obviously in the wrong place, Fhill said.

Then managed a weak smile.

Or. You are right where you need to be.

The proprietor did not smile.

O, I don't think so, Fhill insisted, interesting thrift shop though.

The Lord sighed a cool wind that was deliberately loud.

People looked but they did not see.

There was nothing about the store, nothing that was even remotely thrift.

Hopefully today wasn't going to be one of those days

it would be better to be cloudy and overcast than too much sun.

The owner adjusted the cowl neck of a black form-fitting sheath.

Then placed manicured blue fingers on each hip

of that six-foot-something figure

We don't do thrift here, honey—

And that's when Fhill finally saw how remarkable that mouth, those lips, whether opened or closed.

Mouths were like fingerprints.

Indelible and personal.

They harbored intimacy in the teeth.

And smell of them in the shape.

Fhill'd made a habit of cataloging the ones she'd sucked, or wanted, over time.

Who could forget those electric, sizzling blue lips.

Wasn't this one in her catalog?

Fhill pointed at the mouth

I think I know you. Aren't you Miss Murphy? Didn't you teach

at Junior High School 43?

I don't think we know each other, The Lord said.

Yes, we do! Fhill said. I was a student of yours—

No.

The bass in the voice turned impatient and stormy.

In the LED wall a blue-black cosmic dust sprinkled an image of Earth.

The Lord fiddled with a brass sundial at the counter.
Fhill took a step back.
My apologies, she said, it's just that there's something about—
What we call day is really black beyond the sun. The imposing proprietor
smiled.
And that exquisite mouth, vibrating into tomorrow, spread open
like a book remembering it'd already been cracked to that page.
Fhill turned to go.
Nice to meet you, she said then left.
And so it was

But all that day and the next day and the next, Fhill
thought of little else except The Lord and that delicious, seemingly familiar,
mouth.
It arrested her with its turbulence. Where had she seen it before?

Sometimes she walked by the store but did not go in.
At other times she spied from her side of the street.
Hoping to catch a glimpse of the blue lips and the lacerating tongue of that behexing
mouth

One morning, for reasons she could not fathom,
Fhill awoke in a panic.
She dressed and ran out.
Ran down the street towards the store.
She did not notice how black the day was painted.
And though it was not clear what one thing had to do with another, the store with
the black glass door was gone

This is just not possible!
Fhill shouted at the empty lot that was, in fact, not empty.
Though the human eye is a wondrous tool, a telescope indeed,
there are enigmas the human eye is not built to see.
And no one she asked, no passerby, seemed perturbed.
Some people didn't even remember a store ever being there. ·

After all, if it wasn't a grocery store or a 99-cent store what good was it.
Others said it blinked off and on like the neon sign it was.
So its present absence, the space it filled or left, was of no consequence.
It was, as most remembered it, simply traveling in its own jet stream neither here
nor there

O but it was a mystery, this memory thing.
What was it, really?
Was memory just a filing cabinet in the human brain, storing folders,
bits of information?

Was it a program in a computer performing a wide range of tasks, like forget, re-
call, relive, dream?
Was memory a dimension too tiny, too fleeting to detect? Or
was memory
a possibility that included all possible futures and all possible pasts, including
realities with a totally different physics than
those in our universe?
What was its point, boggled the mind but anyway,
back to the story:

Fhill loved school

School started in September as always.
This particular year Fhill was more excited than usual.
She leapt off the crosstown bus on 125th Street.
Walked several blocks up Amsterdam Avenue and marveled once again
at the four-story building that was Junior High School 43.
Proof, she was grown now.
Fhill looked forward to eighth grade.
She gripped her backpack and joined the stream of new and returning who filed
in that morning

After attendance was taken Mr. Pierce placed manicured fingers
on each hip of that six-foot-something frame

and recited his expectations
of the thirty-odd students in his home room care.
He finished just as the bell rang for first period.
Fhill examined her schedule card.
Subject: Math
Was at the other end of the hall.
On the side of the building that didn't get morning sunlight.
Fhill and her classmates marched inside the shadowed room.
The teacher was at the blackboard writing

$$5 \, (-3x{-}2) - (x{-}) =$$

Please. Sit down. The teacher's back spoke.
Alphabetically. By last name—
The students chattered giggling.
They stumbled over desks to reacquaint with the regimentation that
was school.
Fhill took a seat at the first desk in the last row.
Opposite the window.
The teacher kept writing

$$-4 \, (4x + 5) + 13$$

Then turned around finally

A pair of horn-rimmed glasses pinched the bridge of her nose.
Good morning my flowers, the teacher said. I am Miss Murphy.
Sit up, young man.
Miss Murphy squinted.
The penetrating gaze startled and warned immediately.
It hypnotized the boy.
Straightened in his chair, he looked a foot taller.
Very good, my young scholar, Miss Murphy praised the boy.
You are here to learn, she told the entire class.
And what is learning if not the state of seeding.

And blossoming.
Fhill took note of Miss Murphy's flame blue painted lips. How
blackety black her skin was.
How shiny her afro.
How short she was, how plain.
She might be mean

Miss Murphy pointed at the equations on the blackboard.
These are stories. Which, my flowers, she said, you will learn to read. Now then.
The study of mathematics flourished in Ancient Egypt.
Egypt is on the African continent.
Miss Murphy paused for affect.
Took a long, slow gaze at the faces around the room.
She could see they were loved and less loved.
They were listening now.
Our historians tell us, she told her flowers, Ancient Egyptians were black.
They built the pyramids, based on

TRIANGLES

A   B

and the square root of pi

$$\sqrt{\pi}$$

She said, you black. Never forget that.
Every day there was a new story on the blackboard

Today's story, Miss Murphy said one morning, is the story of a perfect number.
Then she picked up a fresh stick of chalk.
To draw a big white

6

on her spotless blackboard.
A perfect number, she said, is a whole number, not a

$$9.75 \text{ or } 5 \text{ and a } \frac{1}{2}$$

Nor is it funny looking, like the square root of 2

$$\sqrt{2}$$

A perfect number, Miss Murphy lectured, is equal to the sum
of the positive numbers it can be divided by.
Such as

$$1 + 2 + 3 = 6, \text{ which is the first perfect number}$$

She waited. Sucking on her sizable dark lips.
She knew it was too early in the morning for this.
She herself longed to be someplace else.
Arrested by an unbearable anticipation.
Look at them, she thought. They are barely awake.
The one first seat last row stared out the window.
Of course, out there was more exciting.
Yes, but.
This was Advanced Math. And in here, they had a right to these stories.
Even if the stories wouldn't buy them a loaf of bread

The students wrote down in their notebooks what was on the blackboard.
That day they could all say they knew the number 6, but they did not
know perfect.
In their world even smart kids like them knew
eat or be eaten

Miss Murphy regaled her students with her math-stories.
Morning after morning.
She drilled them on the right-angled triangle with its

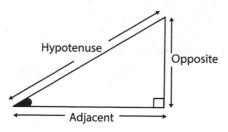

adjacent and opposite and hypotenuse sides.
She quizzed them on the importance of triangles to trigonometry.
And on trigonometry's main functions—*sine, cosine, tangent.*
Which, Miss Murphy instructed, were all simply one side of a right triangle divided by another.
She drew pictures of the unit circle and rotating triangles within it.
And just when the students had begun to understand the triangled stories, there was a whole new story: $a^2 + b^2 = c^2$
Pythagoras's Theorem

By this time though, Fhill had become fascinated with Miss Murphy.
Who believed, she told her students, that curiosity begat discipline.
That the classroom, her classroom, was not a playground.
So, she pushed them.
She pushed them to understand not all mysteries are unfathomable.
She told them they were each beautiful in their own way, a story.
Greater than the sum of their exquisite black parts.
The students were flattered, but they thought Miss Murphy was
a little crazy.
She mesmerized them with that mouth

But neither the students nor any of the other teachers knew much
about Wideline Murphy.
By the gossips' reckoning, why was a woman her age still single.
To them, she acted as if she was better than her own kind.
Preferred, from the looks of it, the company of that mousy Italian woman.
Giovanne Capezzana.
The science teacher.

What could those two have in common.
The gossipers thought small because their imaginations were small.
And so, they couldn't imagine the classroom or the teachers' lounge or passing
each other in the hallway
was foreplay

When the school day was over Miss Murphy and Miss Capezzana exited
the building through separate doorways.
One headed for the bus, the other for the subway.
They each traveled further uptown.
To a prewar building on Riverside Drive.
Where neither of the two women lived where they kept a huge apartment.
Solely for pleasure.
It was always spotless.
The window blinds always drawn.
In the dimmed light the sparse furnishings gave the suite of rooms a lusty muse-
um-quality life.
Just as Wideline, the more fastidious of the two, preferred it

Giovanne arrived first.
She paced back and forth in the bedroom in her black stilettos.
The sun in her generally dark whiteness, luminescent.
Her full hips and buttocks in bondage in the tight black skirt.
Her breasts heaved as she breathed.
She felt them.
Aroused by the wait.
Hardened for suck.
Giovanne felt need for her lover now.
It was only when they were together did she feel acutely alive.
Life, the scientist in her believed, nourished life, in fact.
Life devoured life.
That was its desire.
To be alive by nourishment of another.
Every living thing.
Every cell plant insect.

Every four-legged two-legged and no-legged animal longed for
the body of an other.
For the ecology of touch.
That made life endure, made life survive.
And survival was life's imagination.
No, she and Wideline were not the same, but desire gave birth to their mutual-
ism.
Transformed them, cell to cell, bone to thought, and like math and science,
species to species

Giovanne smoked a cigarette.
Stopped pacing, when finally she heard the key open the apartment door.
Her lover appeared at the bedroom's entrance.
I'm sorry I'm late, Wideline said.
She'd deliberately ignored three uptown trains.
Are you now, Giovanne said.
Yes, I'm so sorry.
Sounded and felt delicious to say.
I don't like to wait.
But Giovanne relished the excruciating uncertainty.
Yes, I know, Wideline said.
Givoanne inhaled a long, deliberate drag of cigarette.
Shall I get the LickHer? Wideline offered. And quickly
she disappeared and returned with it.
Like a benefaction before an altar, deferentially.
Giovanne took the leather-bound riding crop, her eyes on Wideline.
Watched as Wideline's teeth bit her esculent lips.
Then Giovanne expelled what was left of her cigarette into an ashtray
on the night table by the bed.
Wideline undressed and stood naked. She'd waited all day.
The thought of this moment.
Of the release she would feel.
The joy that would be the giving.
Had made her dizzy after lunch.
She'd had to excuse herself from class during sixth period.

The cold water in the teachers' lounge had only produced steam at her neck.
Goosebumps broke out on her arms and legs now.
Giovanne held the LickHer in her teeth like a cat with fresh kill in its jaws.
She wrestled out of her blouse.
Those breasts, Wideline thought.
Then she lay on the bed. Face down.
Si, amore mio, Giovanne crooned. *Sara` dolce*, it will be sweet.
Giovanne gently swiped her lover's ass with the LickHer's floppy tip.
Wideline could hardly wait for her turn to give the pleasure

The first slap broke in the room's air.
Both women gasped.
With each slap, Giovanne alternated again and again between hard and tease.
Slowly, Wideline's member grew.
Hardened.
And Wideline Murphy turned over. Breathing in quick short fits.
She gazed down at herself.
Then up at her lover.
Whose eyes sparkled at the sight of it.
Giovanne tore at her skirt.
To release herself from its constraint.
The LickHer slipped from her hand.
She fell atop Wideline

O, but what about Fhill, you say?
Well then, back to the story:

Once a month Fhill met her friend Overness someplace new.
This spot, Clay's Ark, was Overness's idea.
Of a club it could be said that the alley between two warehouses
on Harlem's Upper West Side was a pop-up in space.
A pair of twins sat on high back bar stools at the alley's entrance.
They wore white lipstick and their skin was neon blue.
They watched in silence as the line moved forward.
Fhill and Overness paid to enter

The alley was without light.

Fhill and Overness pushed their way in.

Beyond the crowd there were no tables or chairs or bar.

Are you kidding me!?! Fhill whined.

Overness tugged at the mini skirt and matching off-the-shoulder floral print blouse.

It was a new outfit, just a bit revealing on that tall frame of his.

It looked good though.

The plan was not to go home alone.

Whenever the topic came up among friends, Overness always avoided what the truth was:

Never been hungered for.

Never had mouth sucked.

Never taken with greedy consent.

What was life without pussy

Think of this as an adventure, Overness said to Fhill.

You never know who's on stage here.

Let's get closer.

Clutching Fhill's hand, Overness slinked through the throng of patrons buzzing near the stage just above their heads.

A barely audible giggle crackled in the dark.

The sound of it surprised.

Fhill looked around for its source.

And soon realized the giggle came from the sky.

Like a meteor, the closer it traveled to Earth, the bigger, louder, more unpredictable it became.

Until, when the racket engulfed the alley, the night itself was laughing hysterically

Overness peeked about, nervous.

People looked skittish.

A thick boy dressed in a navy-blue seamen's outfit edged closer to Overness.

The boy smelled sweet and musky.

He smiled at Overness with a toothy, confident grin.

His nearness calmed Overness immediately

All at once a great dust swarmed over the stage.
It turned blue green.
Then it turned a human shape.
And right before the audience's eyes, the Ever All opened its magnificent, vibrating lips
and swallowed the night's hysterical giggling.
Fhill stared at the stage in disbelief.
There, was the store's proprietor.
With that massive cloud of indigo afro.
That skin.
Black on black through the light of the black before.
That flawless, made-up, black

Hello, Earthlings!
The audience roared and clapped and the store proprietor continued.
I am The Lord. The Lord of Good Pussy. A worker of magicals.
Of mag-wonderous miracles.
Miraculicious wonders and marvelific marvels.
Among my own kind, I am known as a thaumaturge.
So tonight, I bring you messages from the Celestial Carl Sagan—
The Lord's arms embraced the sky—
Who shares with us, and I quote: "Our planet is a lonely speck
in the great enveloping Dark."
At this, the alley, the surrounding streets, the sky above,
encased the crowd in a cold, unknown blackness.
Fhill could not see her hand in front of her.
Overness grabbed for the boy, to feel steady.
The Lord's voice bassed even more in the dark.
"The nitrogen in our DNA," The Lord boomed, "the calcium in our teeth,
the iron in our blood were made of the interiors of collapsing stars."[12]
From somewhere, a single white light illuminated The Lord of Good Pussy

---

12 Carl Sagan, *Cosmos* (New York: Ballantine, 2013), 244.

and a lightning of stars glittered in one of The Lord's hands

For the performer, the package had to be palatable.
This life was littered with the corpses of dark matter, with what was alien—
as humans called whatever came from, was made from, someplace else

Some of the clubgoers jumped up and down like excited children.
They squealed and applauded.
When The Lord squatted and a thunder of planets swam from The Lord's pussy,
they oohed and ahhhed.
Then The Lord said to them, "If you wish to make an apple pie from scratch, you
must first create the universe."[13] So sayeth Carl Sagan, Space Messenger.
So sayeth I.
Fhill trained her eye on The Lord's metamorphic mouth.
Were those lips or labia?
Was that tongue or clit?
Or was this one of The Lord's miraculicious marvelific magicals?

The Lord's gaze swept like a beam over the crowd.
Its laser accuracy picked Fhill out.
We live in a vast, vast knowledge of systems of desire, The Lord said, "Some-
where, something incredible is waiting to be known."[14]
Now The Lord of Good Pussy bent slow and low and into Fhill's face.
Those sizzling blue lips vibrated a breath away from hers.
And just then The Lord's face became a balloon.
It resembled the planet.
Then The Lord whispered, "The vastness is bearable only through love."[15]
Well, at that, Overness broke down and sobbed. Tears
bayoued down Overness's face.
They drew a wetland through Overness's smoky eyeliner and foundation.
Till the streaky mess pooled at Overness's throat. The boy,

13 Ibid., 230.
14 David Gelman, Sharon Begley, Dewey Gram, and Evert Clark, "Seeking Other Worlds"
    (Profile of Carl Sagan), *Newsweek*, Volume 90 (August 15, 1977), 53.
15 Carl Sagan, *Contact: A Novel* (New York: Gallery Books, 2019), 371.

Heaven, put his arm around Overness's shoulder.
The odor from his armpit was sharp.
The scent penetrated Overness's external nostrils and the two interior ones.
It was an infusion.
Aroma therapy to the nervous system.
It eased the secret of chronic alone.
And all the vastness of skin burdened by touch waiting to be known

And then, just like that, The Lord of Good Pussy turned into a weather
cock.
And then was gone.
The swiftness of the disappearance caused confusion at first.
No one knew if the performance was really over.
So, no one clapped or moved or said a word.
As they all stared into the tenderness of cosmic poetry The Lord had made of
this thing called night.
In time, the spell was broken and the clubgoers began to move about and talk
among themselves.
Some, like Overness, had burst into tears.
As this joy had been overwhelming.
Its human beauty simply hurt.
Others wondered if beauty was a human claim only.
To which a faction replied, evolution was an accident and save for accident, hu-
man might never have come to be.
This, they argued, made human life even more precious.
An even smaller faction agreed with the twins at the entrance.
Who loudly proclaimed:
The Lord of Good Pussy came from future.
Whatever, whenever, and wherever that is,
go home

Later, Fhill's silver blue Cadillac convertible slipped through the portal of
after dark.
Overness and Heaven cuddled in its spacious backseat.
Heaven whispered in Overness's ear:

He knew himself to be an old soul, he said.

He didn't want sex only.

He was sure now they'd known each other in another life.

What he felt, unbelievable as it might sound, was love

When the car pulled up in front of Overness's building, Heaven blew Fhill a kiss

as he and Overness vanished inside.

As she drove off, Fhill returned to thoughts of the store proprietor,

The Lord of Good Pussy.

And that phantasmagoric mouth.

Was it Miss Murphy's?

It'd been so many years ago she'd fantasized kissing that mouth.

What had become of the teacher?

Too churned up to go home she let the car drive.

At some point, she thought to call Emma.

Who was good at solving puzzles.

But it was late.

So Fhill steered her car onto the West Side Highway out of the city

The longer she drove, the better she could see.

The light.

In the dark.

Lit tree along the highway upstate.

Lit sleep trailing the few other drivers.

The color of speed.

She could see the coyote in the bush up ahead, clearly.

The badger following near behind it.

The nocturnal synchronicity between them a mutual aid in the hunt for

life that would become food.

Like them, like the stars, she had night vision now.

And though she did not know it straight away, this was possible

because she had seen The Lord of Good Pussy

As she drove, she thought about living in the city.

With its twenty-four-hour pace.

How expensive it was.
Grimy and insatiable.
The desire that was capitalism.
Beat its residents down.
It deprived them of air, space, good drinking water, a more realized life before dying.
The city was a predator.
It ate what it killed.
And for the first time in her life, it occurred to Fhill that she could leave the city for a slower, deeper life among the trees and animals upstate.
She turned around at the next exit.
Headed back to Harlem

Early the next morning, Fhill called Emma.
Hey stranger, Emma said.
Hey baby, Fhill said, you busy?
No, what's up?
I think I ran into Miss Murphy—
Who? Emma said.
That math teacher from Junior High School 43. Fhill giggled.
O really?
Yeah, Fhill said, she's got a crazy shop down the street from me, and she's a per- former too—
No kidding. Hold on, Emma said. I think I hear the family rousing.
A beat later, Emma said, Miss Murphy. Huh.
Seems like one year she was there and the next she wasn't, Fhill said.
There was that petition, remember? Emma said.
Some of the other teachers tried to get her fired.
I don't remember that, Fhill said. For what?
I dunno. I think it was something about ethical behavior, Emma said.
I do remember senior year when Miss Capezzana left.
Miss Murphy told us she was leaving to start her own school—
Did she?
Don't know. Don't you remember me telling you all this?
She was my favorite teacher, Fhill said.

What? She wasn't your teacher, Emma said. She was mine—

Yes, she was. I had Miss Murphy first period, Fhill insisted.

She made me love math.

No, you didn't, Emma said. You were in Mr. Adam's math class next door.

I used to talk to you about Miss Murphy at lunch.

You'd beg me to tell you about Miss Murphy because you had a crush on her.

Mr. Adams bored you.

And so, you failed math.

But I have memories, Fhill said.

Those memories are mine, *cher*, Emma said. Not yours.

But people often believe that the experiences of others are their own—

Gurrl, I can't believe this, Fhill said.

It's all about the brain. The brain has a dynamic, creative ability, Emma said, to not only call up a memory but to revise it.

As a response to new circumstances.

No way, Fhill sounded undone.

It's called revision, Emma said. We revise the stories of our lives over and over in order to arrive at a stable narrative, imagine that—

I'm not sure this is helpful, Fhill said.

Ok. Emma let the moment go. But don't stay away so long.

Your goddaughter needs to see you.

Fhill kept the phone to her ear long after the call was over.

She'd always thought memory was about storage.

But according to Emma, memory was a more complex puzzle.

It was something that was ever evolving, like the self.

Memory was flexible

The sudden urge for a good cup of coffee drove Fhill out of her apartment.

On the street she glanced down the block.

A neon sign blinked on and off

JESUSDEVIL

2.

JesusDevil sat at the table in the center of Fhill's tiny kitchen.
The shape JesusDevil wore, the lazy-eyed look, the sleek, that too pretty,
all made JesusDevil uncomfortable.
JesusDevil wiggled around inside the body.
Adjusted those muscular shoulders.
Cracked the neck.
Took noisy, deep breaths from time to time.
JesusDevil's long, blue digits drummed the small square of the table's top

JesusDevil crossed and re-crossed the lanky legs.
Watched, as the knife she held wavered above the warm cake.
A girlish snort escaped Fhill's plump throat

3.

Fhill cut the sugar-rich lemon poundcake, with cream cheese frosting, in half.
Then in quarters.
Like all the cakes she'd ever made, the cake was lopsided.
Deformed by the warp in her cake pan.
Its aesthetic flaw, she believed, was corrected by the heavy frosting she'd
lumped onto it.
Anticipating the holy sweet of that first bite.
JesusDevil leaned forward as she scooped an enormous piece
onto a small saucer.
Dipped a cobalt-blue pinky-like digit in crumbs flaking the otherwise
spotless table.
Liked that her rust brown body was religiously fat now.
Her breasts barely restrained by the bodice of the understated gray dress.
Made even more noticeable, the trail of buttons from her bosom to her waist
threatening to pop.
Fhill sat down to breakfast eyeing her beloved.

She was not sure if JesusDevil was human or nonhuman or Ever All, the Divine.
But what did it matter what shape love look, smell, or feel like.
She smiled a wide, satisfied grin

In the kitchen's shadow her beloved smelled tart, like morning in an unwashed mouth.
And looked sugary.
The blinding white teeth perfect specimens.
The eyes, their pupils, as black as she believed space beyond the sun.
That she lived *in* space, actually, did not occur to her in the everyday.
Nor did that space had a consciousness of its own.
A vastness, ad infinitum, beyond human calculation.
Of which, what she believed was the Holy, was, in fact,
Breath, its presence, emanating,
as Earth was breathed on by all that was, is, space.
She gave JesusDevil another coquettish grin.
Then felt all a-flurry as she watched that tasting member lick cake crumbs from the pinky-like digit

4.
JesusDevil waited until her own tasting member slid between her lips to meet the cake-filled fork.
Do you really love me, Fhill? JesusDevil said.
Praise God, Fhill sighed. The cake was a perfect sweet.
Ain't I good to you?
My light and my reward—Fhill said.
She reached for more cake.
I shall not want.
She let escape an even deeper sigh.
As JesusDevil's look fondled her.
Until she squirmed and whimpered.
Delighted in the pleasure she gave JesusDevil eating cake
for breakfast, gave her

5.

JesusDevil peered at her nipples.

Have some milk, Fhill baby.

Sweet Jesus, Fhill said.

She lifted the glass to her lips. Swallowed some.

Neatly placed the glass down to the right of the saucer.

Belched.

Then stuffed more cake into her mouth.

JesusDevil's cheeks filled with air.

Imitated, mocked really, the way she looked when she chewed.

Fhill laughed.

Washed down the last bit of cake with the last swallow of milk.

Then she rose from the table.

Made quick work of washing the fork, saucer, glass, and knife.

JesusDevil watched her place them in the plastic dish drain beside the sink

O, by the way, JesusDevil said. Every change in life is a death.

And.

God kills.

But the question is: What comes after God.

So, an afterlife *hah*.

An afterlife is a *hah*. JesusDevil spoke with a halting, staccato, breath.

A someone *hah*.

A someone or a something *hah*.

Who passes *hah*.

into death-life.

a haha hah a hah.

Fhill looked around. What was that?

Just muttering, JesusDevil said.

Praise you, Fhill said.

Fhill stared out the kitchen window absently.

A pair of pigeons fluttered up from below.

The city was a garbage can, and they fed on it.

Much to her distaste.

The Harlem morning was waking now.

She could see lights on in other apartments facing the alley.

She watched her neighbors rise from sleep, their sex, she imagined, reeking

between their legs as they padded to the bathroom, or

to make breakfast for sleepy children off to school.

And then ready themselves for another day of working

lives they did not fully enjoy

At the table, Fhill covered with tinfoil the rest of the cake.

Put the container of milk back in the refrigerator.

Eyeing the cake hungrily as she did so

7.

She went into the living room.

Opened the curtains.

Where light splashed over the dusty candles and bowls of the altar.

Which she'd kept too long.

After *that* love had soured.

Like something abused but forgot at the back of a kitchen cabinet.

She looked at the altar on the table now.

The slip of blue-and-white cloth for Yemaja.

Seashell for Olukun.

A way of life she no longer felt close to

Fhill rearranged plants on the floor beneath the window.

Scooped up a handful of dead leaves.

When she turned around, JesusDevil was right behind her.

She jumped backwards, surprised.

What wonders you perform, she said.

O, I got some wonder for you, JesusDevil said.

And then let the eyes rest on the large gold cross dangling from

the thin chain around Fhill's neck,

into the sweat of cleavage.

Time to go, JesusDevil said.

And protect me inside and out, Fhill said.

She made her way down the apartment's hall, to the closet.
JesusDevil followed behind her.
The body JesusDevil wore danced and writhed.
Ready to rub elbows with life.
To mix and mingle with time, the mirror of ecstasy.
Fhill slipped on her coat and grabbed her keys

8.
The sunless cold bit at her face and legs.
And gave the winter morning its pewter color.
JesusDevil was close at her side.
Crowded her personal space, but so

9.
One night they were on the couch watching television.
When Orrl was five.
Why you have to sit right up under me, Fhill screeched, go sit in *your* spot.
Fhill pointed to the other end of the couch, quasi illuminated by the television's gaze.
Mommie, please—Orrl said.

6.
Orrl was an only child.
In school, she made friends easily.
At home, she was lonely

10.
Please, Fhill sighed. I'm tired.
She was tired.
Of the twelve-hour days on her feet at the restaurant.
Hoping for a decent tip from customers ordering this and sending that back.
All the while that fake smile.
All to make sure they had a roof over their heads.
Something to eat.
A pot to piss in and a window to throw it out

At the other end of the couch, in the spot her mother dictated,
the child trembled.
Sometimes Breath, the unbearable, comes to visit.
Visits you but not you but the person closest to you.
Breath visits, sometimes, as preparation.
As an assault of the seemingly random that is deliberate.
Like a drive-by.
This can be frightening for a child who substitutes you.
How can she know this Breath is not meant for her.
But that Breath is trying out the atoms, the atmosphere, here.
Before coming to you

11.
Orrl's tears washed her cheeks.
She mewed helpless as an animal un-resigned to unbearable captivity

13.
When Orrl reached the age of independence, she said:
I'm moving out.
Fine, Fhill said. Gimme a key. Case of emergency.

12.
At her first job after college, Orrl met Preach.
One of the magazine's senior editors.
Preach had a dandy's style.
She was a woman who took good care of herself.
One day she leaned over Orrl's cubicle.
Wanna go to dinner tonight? Preach said.
Orrl pretended she was busy.
Rifled through a pile of magazines.
Preach waited for a reply.
Orrl gave her some side-eye.
Dinner, Preach said. Just dinner.

14.
Fhill sat on the couch.
She felt light.
Life was sweet now that she'd been in church.
She'd found the intoxicating, the Holy, there.
With which she sang and prayed.
With others.
She prayed for her bills to be paid.
For Orrl, to have the life she wanted.
And a good life for herself.
She prayed for a lover.
She prayed, prayed till tears

Too, there was, these days, the quiet in the house.
A beer or three after work.
Not having to cook if she didn't want to.
Or eat, for that matter.
Watching what she wanted to on television all night if she felt like it

She hit the button on the television's remote.
But the television did not turn on.
Maybe the remote needed new batteries, she thought.
So, she replaced them.
Then nestled, satisfied, on the couch again.
And again, nothing happened. What the hell.
Damnit.
It was almost time for her detective show.
A habit she was religious about.
The show's lead was a hard-drinking loner.
Fhill liked the detective's spicy mind.
And night after night, she imagined herself in the episode:
a chance meeting on the street, a bar somewhere.
The two of them foreplay talking.
In the woman's arms after a case was solved.
What they would do, could do, to each other.

How the liquored breath would smell in heat.
The thought of not having that pleasure upset and unsettled her terribly now

15.
What to do.
For her thrill.
For a television.
If.
Go to your daughter's apartment.
Put the emergency key in the door.
See her on that couch you gave her.
In front of the television.
Drawers hanging off one ankle.
Some woman she calling.
O yes, Preach.
Yes.
Suck.
What.
Daughter begging for fuck.
What.
Who the.
The remote on the floor.
But you want your detective.
Like that

16.
They walked down Adam Clayton Powell Boulevard to 125th Street.
Though still unfamiliar with it, JesusDevil strutted inside the pretty, awkward body.
Holy, the Breath.
Steered Fhill east to Marcus Garvey Park

17.
How many times, months, did she say,
No—don't come over. No.

You grown now, ain'tchu?

19.
Never talk about pussy's desire

18.
The park was desolate.
Its trees, skeletons.
Their skins, blackened with winter's raw, shielded any possibility of growth
being seen.
A dog or two, leashed to a human, poked along the path, nose searching the
morning under frozen leaves, discarded food containers, absent flowers.
Fhill looked around.
Stately brownstones stretched from one end to the other the streets bordering
the enclosed park.
Fhill and JesusDevil turned a bend somewhat obscured by a sculpture of boul-
ders:
Her companion herded her to an empty bench.
And then, itching to get out of that body, disappeared instantly.
A woman materialized beside Fhill

O Holy Jesus! Fhill jumped from the bench.
Well hey, baby, the woman said.
She beamed at Fhill, bright eyed.
The woman wore an expensive-looking coat and shoes too skimpy for the cold.
Fhill eyed her with suspicion.
Do I know you?
I know you ain't forgot *me*, the woman said, I know you ain't forgot Ash.
Ash? Fhill held her breath.
Where was the Holy?

12.
The young and the hip, new to Harlem, upscaled the name to Hansberry's.
But its proper name was Harry Hansberry's Clam House.
In a different time, there were only two items on the menu—raw oysters and boot-

leg whiskey.

Now, the speakeasy-turned-lounge still served oysters, but there was a full bar to accompany its long tradition of live performances nightly.

Fhill had been working at the popular establishment on 133rd, right off Lenox Avenue, a year before Ash came.

She was the head hostess.

She escorted customers to seats at the small round tables.

Chitchatted politely as she settled them in.

Then signaled discreetly for the nearest available server

12.

She couldn't keep her eyes off Georgia Bentley

20.

Who was the pianist there.

The only singer, and a chocolate black.

Georgia was a big, imposing woman.

Partial to performing in her signature white tuxedo with its lavish tails and the matching, elegant, top hat.

One night, after the show and just as Fhill was about to leave,

Georgia called out,

You got somebody at home waiting for you?

Me? No. No, not really.

I didn't think so, Georgia said. Mell and I been meaning to invite you out.

Out where? Fhill sauntered over to the piano.

A friend's place. Not far from here. You'll like it. Georgia looked past Fhill.

A big beauty flowed toward them. Her full-length black boa draped a zebra-print coat that parachuted about her fleshly shape.

Mell stopped in front of the piano.

She urged the woman trailing her, forward.

And introduced her. Hey baby, Mell said, this is Ash. Ash, this is my honey.

Ash is a friend of Hamp's. She needs a job.

A friend of Hamp's, huh? Georgia stood up from the piano.

Well then, welcome home.

Pleasure's mine, Ash said. Her big, bright eyes on the woman standing nearby in the plain, utilitarian-blue coat.

And this is Fhill, Mell said.

Who you need to speak to, Georgia winked at Fhill, if you want a job here.

O, really? Ash looked Fhill up and down.

What are you looking to do? Fhill said. Watched Georgia and Mell slip away toward the dressing room.

Ash's stare felt like a challenge. Any. Thing, she said.

Fhill could see she was an older woman.

And she looked like she took good care of herself.

Fhill shifted her weight from one leg to the other.

Folded her arms in front of her.

Felt something unpredictable.

It flooded her in its silt.

So, what *can* you do? she said.

Everything except dishes, Ash said.

Fhill met Ash's stare with her own.

Of course, she said.

21.

When Georgia and Mell returned, Georgia said, shall we go?

Mell took Georgia's arm.

Ash fell in behind them.

You coming? Georgia said.

Sure, Fhill said.

She looked down at Ash's feet.

Nice shoes, she couldn't help saying. Nice. Real nice.

22.

It was a huge prewar apartment in a building on Riverside Drive.

Ma 'Dam's salon was already heavily attended by the time they arrived.

Hamp greeted them at the door.

Gave Ash a big hug as Georgia introduced Fhill.

Fhill quickly swiped Hamp's look: the penciled mustache.

The gray sharkskin suit shading the slight round of hip.

The white shirt, skinny black tie.

The black Italian loafers with no socks.
Was urbane.
Hamp was Ma'Dam's personal assistant.
And a bulldog at the door.
Hamp directed Georgia through the swarm of people into the living room.
And to its black grand piano

Mell and Ash each grabbed a flute of champagne from one of the roving waiters.
Then pushed their way into the crowded living room.
With Fhill, unsure if she was invited to follow, on their heels

20.
The crowd hooted as Georgia's fingers slowly rolled over the piano keys.
She paused in dramatic fashion.
Winked at a woman nearby, obviously flirting.
Georgia banged the blues she sang into the keys

> *That big girl Rilla*
> *That woman killer*
> *Said that big gal Rilla*
> *That woman killer*
> *She ain't what she seem*
> *She'll turn your woman*
> *To finger-lickin' ice cream*

Then Georgia Bentley pounded the floor with her feet.
Sped up the music's pace.
Stirred the crowd with a different blues, a flow, that was faster and
just as familiar

> *They jus gon' lean*
> *So fresh so clean*
> *For them boys in skirts*

The butch bulge in jeans[16]

She whipped her fans into frenzied abandon.
And they clapped and roared with laughter and appreciation.
And begged and begged, for more

23.
Fhill realized she was alone in the crowd.
After a moment, she struck out in search of Mell and Ash.
Ash, really

24.
There was no sign of the two in the maze of rooms.
Fhill wanted to return to the living room, perhaps even to leave, but was unsure what direction the door was in.
She walked down a hallway into yet another room

20.
There in its unadorned chamber, Mell and Ash huddled on a plush sofa.
They consulted several cards on a table in front of them.
Ma 'Dam, the mocko jumbie in full dress and carnival mask, sat in a plain chair on the other side of the table.
And turned over, just by looking at it, one of the oversized cards.
Ahhh, the VII of Brooms. Ma 'Dam's black eyes grew large under the mask. They squeezed Ash into her pupils.
Face your fears, Ma 'Dam said to Ash. Turn them to your advantage.
By this, you will grow stronger.
And embrace the next obstacle in your path.
Do come in, Ma 'Dam said to Fhill without turning around.
I'm sorry, I was just—
You ok? Mell said.
Yeah. Yeah sure, I'm good. Fhill looked at Ash.

---

16 LaMosiqa, "Sookee, Lex LaFoy & Shirlette Ammons – Purple Velvet Tour Medley," YouTube, https://www.youtube.com/watch?v=vaKrJLDiMwo.

I bet you are, Ash said.

And with that, Ma 'Dam rose up.

Rose fifteen feet in height in one fluid moment.

The legs were unusual even for stilts, the torso proportionately short.

The tarot reader bent a giraffe neck low.

If opportunity comes, Ma 'Dam whispered to Ash, you must cast away
your doubt and pursue it with courage in your hands.

And then Ma 'Dam, with Mell in tow and long, lumbering strides, walked out

6.

So, now that you have found me, Ash said, what do you want?

Fhill looked down at Ash's narrow feet.

They were boney, even.

She wanted to see the toes.

To see how long they were.

If they were polished.

Did they cry out for suck.

I don't know, Fhill lied.

25.

The kiss was hungry.

And noisy.

They slurped each other's mouths like a bowl of soup

26.

There is hunger you will experience only through your nostrils.

Love in which, without, you will be visibly, unalterably, inflamed.

A misfigurement you will recognize in the lover's others.

Who will accost you with how they cry in their sleep.

To live with a saccharine loss.

O, but just to have the lover, the hunger love

20.

Fhill hired Ash as second hostess

27.

Because when Ash took off her shoes, the veins of her feet scalloped across
their surface.

Intricate, delicate.

Like the ve`ve` she painted on the wall above Fhill's bed.

And at the altar, with its melt of blue and white candles and stones and sea
shells she constructed on the table in the living room

27.

At the sight of Ash's feet, those bioluminescent toes especially, Fhill was
overcome.

She fell down on her knees.

Her breath short.

Her eyes rolling back into her head.

Like she'd gotten the Spirit.

She swayed to a holy music only she heard.

She thought of Ash's feet as meant to be prayed to.

Worshipped.

Treated like shrines

28.

Her feet tapered into ankle.

Into calf muscle and knee.

And then thigh.

Into the seat of the panties.

The whiff of which.

Exploded in Fhill's nostrils

28.

Tell me something about yourself, Fhill said.

Why? Ash said.

Why not, Fhill said.

You kind of nosey, Ash said.

I'm in love, Fhill said.

29.

One day it was obvious that Ash was now living in Fhill's apartment

29.

My mother was Haitian, my father said, Ash said. She sold *pwason* and *bannann peze*, fish and fried plantain, on the street in Port au Prince.
Sounds tasty, Fhill said.
I've never cooked her food, not once, Ash said. Anyway.
When my parents met, my father was a sailor.
He wandered the Caribbean.
He was known to women on several of the islands.
This young girl he said move he heart.
He give up sea for she, he said.
Then she die giving me.
And he had to take me to his mother in Dominica.
He die at sea

30.

It dawned on her.
The way Fhill's apartment looked now.
There were no dreams there.
No bridges to the next.
No cliffs to fall off.
The smell of ordinary.
So Ash went to see Ma 'Dam

30.

Hamp answered the door.
And led Ash down an unfamiliar hall to a room Ash had not seen on the first visit

30.

As soon as Ma 'Dam saw Ash, Ma 'Dam rose from the chaise lounge.
And rose, in an instant, to a height that appeared to touch the room's high ceiling.
Ash craned her neck up at the towering figure, if not the very sky.

Ma 'Dam—

Ma 'Dam interrupted, I have already seen the cards.

And a fan of cards appeared face down in Ma 'Dam's hands.

Choose one. Ma Dam bent low.

Ash studied the cards then pointed at the tip of one she could barely see.

The card plucked itself from the spread.

It floated down and hovered in front of Ash's face.

It was the figure of a kneeling naked woman with stars above her head.

That is XVII The Star, Ma 'Dam said. The stars in the sky are like the opportunities in life.

The harder you look, the more there are.

And then, just as fluidly as Ma 'Dam had risen to the heavens, Ma 'Dam descended to Ash's height.

We are only who we are, she said. Who are you?

31.

What are you saying? Fhill said.

I'm done, Ash said.

Done?

With this. Us.

So, you just gon' walk out? Fhill pleaded.

Don't make a scene, Ash said.

And she left, the way she came.

Through the portal that let her in.

With little or no regard for the desires, the vulnerability, of the other.

She wasn't selfish.

This love business was selfish, she thought.

Love was greedy.

It was a harness.

Though it had its perks—company, sex, some security—it was controlling.

And, too often, just a device

9.

Fhill didn't mind being alone.

But there was the constant thud of loneliness without Ash.

The hole.

Left by the anchor.

She was, and felt, abandoned.

Did lonely—like the color of her eyes or her high blood pressure—get passed on, like DNA?

32.

Quite naturally, Fhill was caught off guard.

After all this time.

Not a gray hair, not a pound heavier.

This Ash now was exactly Ash then.

She defied the math of time

This can't be, Fhill muttered.

Looked around.

The park appeared different.

Now, she could see the tiniest buds flowering on the trees.

The barks turning a healthy, proud brown.

The pale over the light lifted.

Right before her eyes the park vibrated with alive in the dead of winter.

Even its breath was sweeter.

Don't be so surprised, Ash said. It's selfish to run from love.

Then she said, I know.

Fhill smirked. O, you do—

Yeah, I do.

Somebody musta broke your heart—

I been lonely, Ash said, since you.

Fhill peered at her. You been lonely?

It's amazing what lonely can teach you.

Ash reached out a hand.

Come, please. Sit with me.

Fhill looked down at Ash's feet.

Her nostrils flared.

For the smell of love.

Its holy breath.

And though she hesitated a moment, Fhill sat down beside Ash, and touched Ash's hand.

And Ash instantly became JesusDevil sitting beside her.

JesusDevil, that boundary crosser, that trickster, grinned inside that ill-fitting skin.

Where is she? Where'd she go? Fhill cried.

She was never here, JesusDevil said. But we, you and I, are incarnate, the Ever All.

Walk with me

1.

And Fhill, too confused to speak, too hungry for love, too difendated,[17] obediently followed JesusDevil as, hand in hand, they headed in the direction of her daughter's apartment

---

17 Difendate [die en date] *verb*: 1. To be aroused by the memory of desire but not the subject of it. 2. To not want what is wanted. Word created by Alexis De Veaux, www.livingdictionaryproject.com/inventedwords.

THE WAKE

It was the future now.

She walked along the beach picking up discarded plastic trash, stuffed the sack
of it over her shoulder.

In a time she needed order and was obsessed with cleanliness, she scooped up
litter like a maniac.

On the subway platform.

Newspapers blown haplessly down the street.

Empty bottles and cans dropped at a curb, and who cared that the Earth was
getting dirtier and dirtier.

Wasn't hard to see

Over her shoulder a black-and-white whale swam to shore.

Fhill stopped, dumbfounded.

The behemoth let the calf slide like a gift from its mouth, the gift
into waist-deep water lay there listless.

The bigger mammal was exhausted.

The child had died one half hour after birth.

The mother had lifted the child's sinking body to the surface repeatedly, repeat-
edly willing the life.

Every time the child sank, the mother moved air between the nasal sacs in her
blowhole.

She whistled and clicked and groaned low frequency pops to her family swim-
ming nearby.

What is happening in the water

Seventeen days.

One thousand miles, in the water, emaciated baby the mother balances
on her head, the four hundred pounds.

Pushed through the ocean, the dead female baby.

Each time she sinks, the mother hoists baby out of water.

Takes a deep breath, repeats.

Refuses to let go the future of the clan the whole way.

All of them grieving.

The mother refuses to let her precious sink to the bottom,

to decompose

out of human sight

Nestled close to the baby.

Who would have expected this.

Who, on a Monday morning clear as possibility.

Sky dotted with puff cloud.

Only a few sunbathers here and there on the beach.

The weekend crowds gone with their feral children, their pale bodies slathered in sunscreen, all that noise.

Was reason to avoid the city's beaches.

Was the reason for so much debris.

And soon as the sunbathers saw the orca whale, they pointed and shouted and ran towards it with cell phones.

Took selfies with the orca in the background suffering like it was this mother within range of Fhill.

The humongous cetacean, breathless.

What had surfaced was clearly distress.

And those humans just stood there, gawking.

This was, indeed, they agreed, the arrival of the alien.

It was just frightening.

The way the sea opened in the sky

Then some of the sunbathers ventured their hubris into the water, surrounded the mother as they splashed her with the sea.

Fhill wondered why.

The sea licked at the orca's body.

As it brushed her with soundless waves.

And that, too, leaped the ordinary.

Is a wave a wave without its voice?

What is any life form without its preternatural pitch?

The sea was too calm, Fhill thought looking at its surface.
But looking underneath, way way down and down even further than human or
the deepest diving whale,
and the last trickle of sunlight,
where Olokun lived in secret,
there were underwater deserts.
Can you imagine?
Schools of fish suiciding in the watery depth

The sea was not calm, it swallowed.
And right here the Orca blinked, and Fhill dropped the sack of beach garbage
and yelled,
STOP.
STOP THAT.
And the water throwers, much to their surprise, looked at her and saw
unreadable and big lips and the dreaded hair tentacled like sea anemone.
And backed up, cautiously.
They studied Fhill.
Then the thing in the water.
And spoke without speaking, *these animals are dangerous they stick together.*
Then, they stepped away slow as possible so as not to startle the creatures.
As Fhill beached herself there in the sand.
To sit with the mother and the body at the shore

In time the sunbathers went home, to dinner and TV.
As the tide came in and the earth turned dark.
But further out on the ocean, a fishing boat sat in the water still as silhouette,
its steel cables in a block and tackle system over the deck.
Outlined a family business and generations, the ocean gave them breath.
Now the crew of four in rubber skins and the captain, pulled up the last catch in
the bounty swollen nets.
Fish wriggled and flopped about out of water on just enough air before their gills
and scales dried up.
The crew congratulated each other and raised a beer to the captain, after throw-
ing back fish too little to sell.

And before they put a ton of dead fish on ice.
As the small family boat returned to shore, bleeding in its wake

Later that night, and O, it was much later, when heaven was its blackest above
Fhill, a paradise of stars watched from the Milky Way there.
And there appeared the constellation Cetus, once the sea monster, now heav-
en's whale.
In the region not far from other water constellations—
Aquarius and Pisces and Eridanus.
Eridanus, at the galaxy's edge near the supervoid that was perhaps the imprint
of another universe.
As Fhill stared into the chilly dark and felt them before Three Medicines material-
ized at her feet.
They looked human but they were not quite

You can't just sit there, said the most puckered. Scales for a face.
Who are you? Fhill asked.
You must celebrate, the seagull headed said.
Celebrate the life, said the one with fins.
What are you? Fhill insisted.
A portal through, offered the finned. Do you pray?
As a matter of fact, truth was Fhill had not prayed in quite some time having
abandoned the astrology of belief.
Well, do you? the gull asked.
And being that it was dark there at the ocean, and she was alone and hungry,
and, sure, now she was seeing things, and she knew how, even if she hadn't late-
ly, Fhill bowed her head in prayer.
Then Three Medicines quietly sat down in the sand and watched over Fhill, the
mother whale, and corpse of baby swaying in the attraction between Earth and
low full Moon that was the tide.
All through the night.
And all through the night Fhill prayed

When morning came the sun bled, a blistering orange on the horizon's line,
the deep out there an impenetrable lapis that became icy blue at the shallower

shore.
Fhill awoke alone on the beach.
The dead calf was there, the mother was gone.
Fhill searched this way and that and up and down the beach.
Her eyes scanned the ocean, but the water kept secret when and how
the mother left.
The sight of the baby's corpse alone like that now suddenly filled her with grief.
And grief filled her with sadness.
But how could she grieve a life she had not known.
Was grief the portal through which memory comforted the living but disturbed
the flight of the dead?
As the dead became prayer.
As to mourn was to suffer loss of the physical, and grief was the terms of rela-
tionship

But what was the relationship here?
Why didn't the mother Orca just let the carcass sink to the ocean's floor where
the dead were, as was natural, eaten by the living at the bottom?
Where life recycled the dead and everything down there is an organism belly full
of other organisms.
In the ocean, though not on its floor, the fish we eat now are fish that were eaten
by fish in the cycle of time.
Fish eat fish that ate our ancestors in the ocean, and
we—cannibals—are recycled from the dead

O, it was a terrible feeling this feeling of grief that Fhill took home with her and
brought back to the beach with bottles of water and bottles
of wine and cheese sandwiches for the feast like a prayer,
which she shared with the small crowd of empathics that had grown now
near the still body.
And so, they all drank and ate and told each other tall tales about
gigantic sharks and killer whales.
All except for Fhill.
Who took off her clothes and walked naked down to where the baby corpse lin-
gered, and entering the sea, bit by bit, she bathed.

Especially her armpits and breasts and between her legs.
And then her head, four times, turning once in each direction until her body absorbed the sea's salt

Until the sea's salt sweetened her skin.
And when that part of her ritual was done, she
plunged into the water fully and began to swim away from shore just
as a lone seagull alighted atop the orca's carcass.
It pecked at the skin, tentative.
Then it pecked and pecked with more confidence before it flew up to circle
the potential.
Before it flew away as if, like the gods' own breath,
it had never been there

As Fhill swam out further and further.
Until she entered the part of the sea that was the deep, where the water was a
wild, dark lapis.
And she took a breath.
And went under then, and in the silence of the water, lo and behold, she discovered she had gills.
Like other fish do.
And she felt something, something more than being thirty feet down or an embrace
or the shapeshift of being fish but.
Something.
So, she swam back up to the surface and back to shore.
And when she reached land, she was breathing through her lungs again, naturally.
The seagull was back atop the dead orca, accompanied now by several noisy
others who feasted on the decaying meat

While over the next several days as Fhill and the other empathics peeked at the
body from time to time and danced and came and went for more bottles of wine
and more bottles of water and baskets of cheese sandwiches until,
drunk and satiated,

they were too tired to dance anymore,
too exhausted to say out loud: *as life in the sea dies, we die too*

Well, by now, the whale carcass had become malodorous and some
tired of the smell.
And the beach authorities were called in to do something about it.
The beach authorities called Animal Removal and Conservation.
Which took its time, after all, dead animals were already dead though
Baby Orca was life to the microscopic feeding above and below her

In the cycle of life above and below us, we are all just food.
Which is what Fhill thought when, full of built-up gas and putrid smell, the car-
cass exploded on the beach.
Its huge entrails like an army of snake slithered into the water.
Of course, this was natural for a decomposing whale body, but people at the
beach screamed and covered their eyes.
Until Fhill herself screamed, LOOK. LOOK THERE

Way out in the ocean the mother whale came up like a spectacle shedding wa-
ter.
She came up and went down and up again.
This terrifying that lived beneath.
Went down again, and with all her might and beauty, she shot up once more.
And the massive torpedo of her hung in the air, suspended for what seemed
impossible to the people watching.
Before she disappeared from their sight, way below.
And watching the great spray of sea that Orca Mother left behind, it came to
Fhill.
This was what the mother had wanted all along.
To have life
in the water
seen

LIFE (NOTES)

The microbe communicated with her.

Through the fever.

In the terrible muscle and body ache, she woke up with that morning.

She hadn't been able to smell food.

Or the fresh flowers on her dining table.

Or her own body.

Nothing, for days.

The absence of that ability startled her.

The night before, when Emma lay in her bed.

And Emma had said, gimme some suck baby.

And when Fhill willingly went down but she couldn't smell the pussy

On her way to the clinic, the outside world was unearthly quiet.

The streets along the route were barren.

Abandoned cars sat in a gaunt layer of dirt and absence.

Nothing moved, save for the lone car ahead of her.

Fhill drove with a feeling, a disturbance, in her gut.

Something was not right.

Her body was off

A couple of hours later the results of her RBR—Rapid Body Reading—confirmed
the microbe, the O, had attached to her cells.

Reproducing at a fast pace.

She had become a host.

Living with and in relation to symbiosis with a microbe that was neither alive
nor dead as humans defined that binary.

The microbe, this virus, existed in a third reality of being, which was neither life
nor death but an existence within which it could appear "alive" when
it attached itself and reproduced in its host's cells.

And appear "dead" when it did not.[18]

According to the doctors at the clinic, humans had never seen this microbe before.

Though, they believed, microbes—viruses—had lived on the planet billions of years, billions before the human came.

Some kinds of microbes were already living in human hosts.

They were essential to human health and human life.

But this microbe, this O, had a different intelligence.

Why it had made itself known, why it *wanted* to be known, now, was unclear

The attending nurse was outfitted in a hazmat suit and protective gloves.

You're one of the fortunate ones, the nurse said to Fhill.

You won't need a ventilator, you can breathe on your own, not like some.

The nurse's eyes indicated the overcrowded waiting room, the people coughing and wheezing and begging for breath.

I feel horrible, Fhill acknowledged.

We don't know what this thing is, the nurse sympathized. And we're not prepared for it. Painkillers are the best we can offer right now.

Fhill walked to her car, dazed.

Feverish.

How had this happened?

Did she catch it at the food market?

When?

Was it when she'd stopped to get gas?

To talk with her neighbors, when?

Hadn't she followed the city's rules for The Sheltering:

Go out only for food, medicines, medical emergencies.

Do not go out without face covering.

No human contact.

But still.

She felt lightheaded.

---

18 See Carl Zimmer, *Life's Edge: The Search for What It Means to Be Alive* (New York: Dutton, 2021).

Wasn't sure where she was for a moment.
The clinic's parking lot pulsated.
And she thought she saw the clinic's veins, its heart.
She shook her head violently.
And the image left her eyes.
But the unsettling vision left her shaking.
She barely made it to her car

Unbelievable, Fhill shouted as she turned the Cadillac on.
I'm a goddamn host. Unbelievable.
But it was not

By the twenty-fourth month of The Sheltering.
The microbe had passed first between humans by touch.
It'd taken months before the kissing and the hugging and the handshaking had stopped.
Months before humans accepted they were now living with a something different.
Before they locked themselves indoors.
And the city's buildings and sidewalks were mysteriously graffiti-ed with the microbe's nickname, The M.U.C.K, the mutating, unpredictable, confusing, k-os

At home, Fhill crawled into bed.
She waited for her daughter's image to appear on her computer's screen.
It had become the only way to visit safely

Orrl stared at her mother.
You should've asked me to go with you—
I didn't want to be a bother, Fhill said.
Orrl lifted an eyebrow. Fhill, what is the point of your constant hyper independence?
I don't need to feel more shame, Fhill said.
You didn't do anything wrong, Orrl sounded tender. Sorry.
I got sick, Fhill countered, I got the O.
The fear rose on Fhill's face.

And so far, you're living with it, Orrl said.
Yeah, but hundreds of thousands have already died being hosts, Fhill stared
back at Orrl

It was the only thing on the news these days.
Some people thought bats and pigs were the first hosts.
Among the N Virons there was widespread belief the planet's defenses had been
disturbed by thousands of years of terraforming.
This, they contended, with its attendant evidence—human created plastics, con-
crete, and aluminum—had disturbed the biosphere.
And eventually ended up in rock layers of the Earth.
What had been below Earth's soil and crust, they admonished now, was
above ground, host shopping.
Well, what goes around comes around, the Long Livers warned.
In their own language, the Logicians agreed:
They viewed the current geological age as a period during which
human activity
had been the dominant *and* the dominating
influence on the planet.
The human had had an adverse, an altering, effect
Was extinction, or mutation of the human species, a possible correction?

Yes, Orrl's voice was flat. Hundreds of thousands have died.
But some have not, Fhill.
She waited a beat.
They call themselves The Thrivers.
Fhill squinted. The who?
The ones whose lives, Orrl hesitated, changed.
They didn't die? Fhill said.
They didn't die.
And then, after a moment, Orrl said, maybe death isn't the point.
I have no idea what you talking about, Fhill said.
She felt the achy pain again. Reached for the bottle of painkillers.
That's what they gave you at the clinic? There was accusation in Orrl's tone.
Supposed to help, Fhill swallowed two capsules, dry.

The O likes that stuff, gets high off of it, Orrl said.
Fhill turned from the answer-for-everything she heard in her daughter's mouth.
You seem to know a lot about this thing.
My heart's mate, Leaf, is one of The Thrivers—
O yeah? Fhill wasn't interested.
Yeah. I've gone to the gatherings, Orrl said.
The painkiller was swift in its effect. I'm tired, Fhill said.
She felt pleasantly relaxed, as if she'd had a good joint.
But she wasn't sure if she or the microbe was high.
And, she was feverish.
O God, Fhill said.
Mom. Listen—
Some other time, Fhill cut off her screen

Over time, the fever remained.
Whenever Fhill took her temperature it was always at 102.2 degrees.
Though she felt uncomfortably warm all the time, her body was adjusting to living with fever.
But it had a low tolerance for the way the microbe spoke to her.
The sudden pain seized the muscles in her shoulders and back.
The pain disfigured her fingers and toes with cramps.
It made her scream and gasp for air.
Between Fhill and the microbe, the language they spoke was pain.
It was excruciating

Soon Fhill learned she could sedate the microbe with the clinic's drugs.
But when the high wore off, she'd hear from the O, in its sudden and searing
tongue

Without an ability to smell, her life orbited an unfamiliar dimension.
In the kitchen, the barely used refrigerator pussed with dead leafy greens and
rotting lemons swathed in a blue-green mold.
Her multigrain bread turned black.
Several cartons of strawberries suffered a grayish-white fungus.
And cheese, once a favorite, became pocked with green craters.

What had once been alive, her food, was now dead.
And she wondered.
What is life?
What is death?
Is death the ibeji, the twin, of life?

Though she looked in the refrigerator often out of habit, she became detached
from the comfort of its contents.
She no longer got pleasure from food.
Or from her rosewater bath salts.
Or fresh air blowing in through the window.
Life without smell was a disorienting sensation that left Fhill blank

One day Fhill lay down for an afternoon nap.
She closed her eyes.
To her surprise, she could see every detail of her bedroom with her eyelids shut.
Immediately she opened them and blinked at the room.
But nothing had changed.
And though it took a while, she soon closed her eyes again.
And again she saw her bedroom clearly, even though her eyes were closed.
She snapped up, at the edge of her bed, frightened.
How was this possible?
How was it possible to see like that?
Was she actually seeing or simply having a memory?
Was memory just a filing cabinet in the human brain, storing folders, snacks
of information?
Was it a program in a computer performing a wide range of tasks like forget, re-
call, relive, dream?
Or was memory a possibility that included all possible not-yets and all possible
has?
She didn't know.
But she knew this much: she had seen *how* she had seen.
Incredible as that was

The months of The Sheltering dragged.

As did the loneliness, the days in isolation.

Fhill found herself at the window often, staring at the nothing outside.

If a car went by, or better yet, some lone soul on foot, her eye would follow the evidence of life hungrily, longing.

She ached for company.

Humans are not meant to live like this, she screamed at the evening news night after night.

And night after night, as quiet stalked the lifeless streets, as quiet snaked under her front door, curious as an unwelcome guest, lonely became Fhill's live-in companion

As the ability to smell continued to elude her, Fhill's eyesight evolved.

Not only could she see with her eyes closed.

She could see colors impossible to see simultaneously.

Like red-green that was not the dull brown of the two pigments when mixed.

But a color its own that was somewhat like red and somewhat like green.

And that yellow-blue she saw when day broke.

Which was not green but a shade of light akin to yellow and to blue.

She saw colors the human eye had no names for.

Colors, light frequencies humans cannot actually see

And although this was staggering enough, indeed, it was seeing the sun that utterly astounded her.

To look at it directly, with her naked eye.

To see the sun, immense.

A ball, blazing and luminous.

The skin of the sun, its visible surface.

Pulsed and morphed before her eyes.

As granules of rising gas gave it the speckled look of orange peel. O, this monstrous beauty.

This breathtaking.

This local star, terrified Fhill. Yes it did.

Terrified Fhill to look at it.

And the looking hurt.

But she soon discovered she could not help herself.

She wanted, she craved, the sweet of that.
Like an addictive drug.
The hurt was as pleasurable as it was brutal

O, but to set a human eye on the atmosphere above the sun's surface.
And beyond that, upon its outer atmosphere.
Where the sun, flares.
And which gradually transforms into solar wind that flows out to greet the
solar system, black as space beyond this sunlight.
In a consciousness of its own.
A vastness, ad infinitum, beyond human calculation.
Which was, Fhill did not know, the Breath of Presence in the sixth dimension.
Where space multiplied time.
And where her eyes were telescopes that could see, in the black otherworld,
when she wanted to,
the death and birth of stars

One day, the pain in her body was gone at last.
It was a signal the microbe, the O, had accepted her.
And though her eyes looked the same as they always had, Fhill began to believe
they appeared different now.
Even in the house alone, she hid them behind thick-framed sunglasses.
It was one more layer of difference.
And, as it was in her reality, difference carried with it, shame

Gathering with others was illegal now.
The Thrivers came together in secret.
In one of the many houses abandoned after the hurricane.
At the edge of an abandoned neighborhood.
Fhill stood beside Orrl in what would've been someone's living room.
The corpse of a sofa decomposed against the window.
Wallpaper peeled everywhere.
She could hear a rat or two scamper back and forth inside the walls.
I don't know why I let you talk me into this, Fhill said under her breath.
Try to be patient, Orrl said.

She watched as others filed into the room's semi dark.

Laid eyes on a figure circling the edges of the gathering.

Leaf, she called out, Leaf! Over here!

A blue kaftan opened like a parachute around Leaf as Leaf followed the sound of Orrl's voice.

The stubby blueback dreadlocks writhed with a slight movement.

Leaf's indigo black skin was iridescent.

Leaf gave Orrl a long tight hug.

Fhill, Orrl said, this is my heart's mate, Leaf.

O! Fhill took a step backwards. Stared at the face that was smooth of eyes.

Leaf exclaimed, Ahhh, the mother of my heart.

Fhill's a Thriver, Orrl said. I'm sure of it now.

Leaf's dreadlocks bowed in deference.

Leaf put a hand on Fhill's shoulder.

I see, Leaf said to Fhill.

Who could not stop staring.

I'm sorry, I don't understand. You see?

Yes. I have touch, Leaf said. We have all lost a sense and gained a hyper one, just like you.

Fhill turned to Orrl. You a Thriver too?

I wish, Orrl said, but I haven't been given that gift.

Which comes from the O, Leaf rubbed Orrl's back.

With an anxious look on her face, Fhill adjusted her sunglasses more than once.

Looked around.

The gathered moved about.

There was an air of strange enveloping them.

They seemed a beat or two out of time.

As some came to greet Orrl and Leaf, Fhill sensed the intimacy between them.

It was comforting.

When she noticed the balding, dark-complected dandy in a gray sharkskin suit.

Bent over and moving, with an easy permission, from one butt to the next.

Until what was to be known about diets, about emotions—written in the biographies of odor and pheromones—was not called a gender.

For The Thrivers were not known to each other as *she* or *he* nor *they* nor *them*.

These ideas, they'd agreed, were from another, a previous world that they had
now to shed

Fhill became agitated when the dandy bent behind first Leaf then Orrl.
I don't want my ass sniffed, she whined.
Whiskey just wants to get to know you, Orrl said.
Whiskey can no longer hear, Leaf chimed in. Whiskey reads our world through
the nose.
Fhill sighed. What had she gotten herself into. Animal behavior and
other human activities, she said aloud.
Eyed Whiskey.
Who gave her a warm smile, then circled behind her.
Bent down and nosed her butt, closely.
The odor of fear and unfamiliarity leaked from her.
Whiskey padded away disinterested in knowing any more

In the middle of the gathered, a small person, head lowered in a meditative bow,
sat on a bench in front of a portable keyboard.
That's Ash, Orrl directed Fhill's attention.
So far, Leaf said, Ash is the only one who has lost three senses. Sight, taste, and
smell.
The gathered hooted as Ash's fingers slowly rolled over the piano's keys.
Ash paused in dramatic fashion.
Then, in a rich dirty bass, Fhill felt the thunderclap of in her chest, Ash sang the
blues into the keys

> *We are The Thrivers*   *ba boom*
> *We are The Thrivers*   *ba boom*
> *More than survivors*   *who whom*
> *We'll bend the time*
> *Like a blues sublime*

Ash's feet pounded the floor, stirred the crowd, sped up the music.
And the gathered hooted and stomped with a frenzied abandon.
They sang along

We more than succumb   *ers*   *ba boom*
We more than survive   *ers*
We is The Thrivers
We is The Thrivers
O yeah
O yeahhh
we is

Fhill peeked at Orrl and Leaf laughing and holding hands.
They lived with and without the microbe.
Here, they were clothed in intimacy and their people.
And their people, like her, were no longer just human.
Like her, they were something other than, more than

THE NIGERIAN WOMAN'S DICK

It was in a time in New Orleans.

A city that shared a rebellion narrative, an origin story if you will, with other black geographies: New York City; Durham; Tulsa; the colony San Miguel de Gualdape in 1526.

It was known to its inhabitants (though they had no need to say aloud) as a geography where black people lived, but not the word impossible.

As when a noun becomes a verb

And there lived in this time, a Nigerian Woman.

Who awoke one morning after a deep sleep.

It was gone again.

It was nerve-racking how the statue came and went.

At will, it seemed.

To the Nigerian Woman, it did what it pleased.

Without regard, apparently, for the distress it caused her.

Which finally drove the Nigerian Woman to her good friend's door,

in the sweltering heat that morning

The peephole latch clicked.

With a frown, Fhill opened her door.

What? Fhill said, with nothing on except a half-buttoned white shirt.

My sister! I need your help, the Nigerian Woman said.

I'm a little busy right now, Fhill said.

O? said the Nigerian Woman, who went by the name Aguta. Peeked over Fhill's shoulder.

Who is here with you—

None of your business, Fhill said.

So, we are keeping secrets now? Aguta folded muscular, tattooed arms in front of his attrahent breasts.

The Nigerian Woman was a towering man.

In a pink kaftan.
Pink colored her mustached lips.
And dangled in teardrop earrings.
Aguta had not shaved.
The deliberate stubble was flecked with gray

Ok, my sister, ok. But—Aguta pointed a bejeweled finger as he backed away—
I leave you with the words of my good friend Mr. Chinua Achebe: "That we are
surrounded by deep mysteries is known to all but the incurably ignorant."[19]
In truth, Aguta had never met China Achebe.
But he thought of the celebrated and outspoken Nigerian novelist as an open
window through which the proverbs of his culture came in like fresh air.
And because he was a conduit for air, Achebe was a friend

Fhill sniggered and shut her door.
But she knew Aguta did not like to be ignored, for indeed, he was a dependable
friend.
He'd paid her overdue rent on more than one occasion.
He'd penetrated her, hard and quick, as she'd asked him to, while wearing a
dress.
He never asked for anything.
But he was Queen of the long and narrow double shotgun he and Fhill lived in
side by side, she knew that.
So, it was no surprise the following morning when Aguta knocked again

Fhill opened her door a crack.
Was just enough to see she was naked this time.
The Nigerian Woman pushed open the door and swept pass Fhill.
His blue kaftan ballooned behind

Inside, Fhill's place was still.
Her house hadn't awakened yet.
A hand jutted out from the first room, a robe dangling from it.

---

19 Chinua Achebe, *Anthills of the Savannah* (New York: Anchor Books, 1998), 93.

As Fhill reached for the robe, Aguta rolled his eyes.

Then he spun around quick as a flying cat.

He spun out the door and back to his place.

What is going on? Fhill demanded.

She stood in Aguta's doorway.

I am at the end of the rope, Aguta confessed.

Why? Fhill asked.

Aguta sighed. I need tea.

So, he brewed a pot of lemon balm.

As he relayed this story to his dear sister:

As you know, Oya has been my family's orisha for generations.

When my dear mother, for whom I was daughter, went to the ancestors, Oya
came for me.

To keep her close, I made an altar right there—Aguta pointed to the corner of the
room where an empty space, a hole on the floor, was surrounded by an earth-
enware pot, a machete, brown glass beads spilled among red ones, and a
freshly lit purple candle.

One day she is here, Aguta continued, the next she is gone.

Fhill eyeballed the spot where the statue usually stood.

Then Aguta.

Then the empty spot again.

She glanced about.

Maybe he'd moved it, maybe it was just misplaced.

Aguta sipped his tea.

I cannot tell you how she goes. Or where.

The Nigerian Woman sighed then turned to Fhill.

Oya is gone, my sister, what shall I do?

And with that, the Nigerian Woman sobbed into his tea.

His tears turned the pungent liquid solid, and eyeing it carefully, she put her
teacup down.

As she'd come to know lately that everything in life could not be understood

Fhill felt sorry for Aguta.

Truth be told though, she had something else on her mind.

That unfinished business in her bedroom.

But seeing Aguta in such a state she quietly said, I cannot help you sister
but I know someone who can.

And later that morning Fhill introduced the Nigerian Woman to her bedroom
company.

This is Theme. Theme Le Roy, Fhill said. A private detective.

The detective was an indigo black, her skin iridescent.

Her stubby blueback dreads writhed with a slight movement.

She wore a three-piece gray sharkskin suit.

O, my! Aguta shrieked. A private dick!

Theme gave Fhill some side-eye. Then grinned.

Which made Fhill want.

The detective took a small notebook and expensive-looking pen from her jack-
et's inside pocket.

Let's start from the beginning. Theme Le Roy pursued the matter at hand

The Nigerian Woman scrutinized this detective.

Seemed a bit aloof, really.

Absent of warmth.

Like a piece of information that presents itself as objective reality.

And calls itself fact.

Which suggests true.

But what is true travels a slippery binary.

Some facts are false.

Well ... The Nigerian Woman sat in a chair and sucked a dramatic breath.

When one is born, she began, we say one chooses a head.

And is then endowed with a cosmic essence, the soul's matrix.

This essence can be experienced in its natural manifestation, its spirit form.

As water or wind, as fire or tree.

Theme looked up from a scribble of notes.

This magic wasn't the usual kind.

The magic she was accustomed to boiled in her blood.

It had an insularity to it.

But she'd long wondered what other magics, otherwheres, might be possible

Aguta kept talking.

We do not worship these as such.

We worship them as the loci of beings we call Orisha.

In one's family, the Orishas are a shared ancestral legacy.

And because she was overcome, Aguta stopped talking just then.

She got up from his chair and knelt at the Orisha's empty spot.

Aguta whispered a language neither Fhill nor Theme understood.

When he was done, the Nigerian Woman lit another purple candle.

Sucked in a loud breath.

Then returned to his chair.

After a moment the detective asked, Can you describe this Orisha?

You will see she is a statue, Aguta said.

Very tiny, Fhill chimed in. Then indicated with her hand low to the ground.

Yes, Aguta said, her breasts are small as well.

Aguta's hands pressed against the bulge of his own.

She wears a necklace, and a flat crown in the shape of an M.

Anything else? Theme said scribbling.

She's made of bronze, Fhill offered.

So, she's expensive, Theme said. Any chance someone came in here and took her?

Aguta protested. Oya disappears and Oya appears. At will. Oya has destroyed my peace. *Eepa Heyi*! What a goddess!

Yes, Theme said matter-of-fact.

But what were the facts here?

Was the evidence of disappearance the empty hole, that was, it seemed, visible?

Were the facts and the mystery enveloping those facts, antithetical?

A life of shadowing mysteries had shown Theme Le Roy that facts could, often did, contradict each other.

As such, they could be competing truths.

Though contradiction did not define truth, she knew that.

To search for *the* truth was to search for an absolute.

Competing truths or facts were useful to shaping complexities rather than absolutes.

Verifying facts was another story.

That often meant Theme had to be subjective rather than objective.

That way she could see facts as artifacts

And the context and argument for them as copartners of facts.[20]
On the one hand, the improbable was always possible.
On the second hand, a private investigator was like any other researcher—
a dog with a bone.
On the third hand, there was this state of being improbable, of being both this
and that.
This state of being lively numinous, was something Theme Le Roy intrin-
sically understood

One day, after she'd turned drinking age, Theme walked into The Fabulous.
A neighborhood bar between neighborhoods.
Some folk sat around the long purple bar chatting and drinking.
Preach, Queen! was sitting cross legged on a bar stool.
His lecture was in full swing:
Y'all know whatumsayin.
Y'all know whatumsayin.
And I ain't the first.
The first was the late and brilliant Barbara Christian.
Let me bring some history up in here.
Rise up, Barbara Christian black feminist.
Most of our mothers, some of our daddies too, is black feminist.
They may not call themselves that but.
Ask them bout rent.
Ask them bout kale and collards before hip.

Ask them bout those piss-ass jobs.
Bout what we call theory in the flesh—
Preach, Queen! paused while the bartender, Overness, poured him another
whiskey.
Theme inched towards the less occupied side of the bar.

---

20 Alexis De Veaux, *Warrior Poet: A Biography of Audre Lorde* (New York: W.W. Norton, 2004), xiii–xiv.

She sat next to two men.
Preach, Queen! sipped his drink then smacked his lips.
Though his government name was Nugent Baldwin Beam, he liked
that he was known here by a different persona.
In the university's whiteness, where he was the tenured Professor Beam and
specialized in Black Geographies,
he was the Invisible Man.
But here and loved, he exercised his skills in the service of his people.
That PhD was only a tool to a life without lack.
It was freedom.
For himself and for all those who looked like, talked like, thought, and fucked
like him outside a box

Ask your people what power is, what it ain't. Preach, Queen! signified.
Sheeeet, somebody let out.
They'll tell you. They'll tell you, from they own understanding. Preach, Queen!
let his tears flow.
They own understanding.
Of the multiple, the simultaneous ways we been *beat* down.
Beat on.
Beat up.
And we *still* making beauty—
A woman in big round sunglasses testified, Y'all don't even know!
Preach, Queen! one of the men sitting next to Theme hollered.
O, don't get me started, Preach, Queen! answered, but let me raise up some
history.
Because Barbara Christian was a prophet.
I know y'all know what a prophet do—
Speak in tongue, a man replied.
Y'all know whatumsayin. Barbara Christian wrote it.
Our people do *do* theory.
We know how to theorize.
We know how to thee-o-rize, Overness slid a flirty hand over her bald head,
tugged at her bowtie and strutted about.
To the delight and witness of the bar's patrons.

At last, Preach, Queen! laid eyes on the newcomer

Well, what have we here?
He directed the room's attention to the blue-black stranger.
His smile was big, toothy.
Genuinely welcoming.
He'd said *what* instead of *who* on purpose, Theme sensed.
Overness appeared with a fresh bottle of whiskey and an empty glass.
She poured a drink and pushed the glass in front of Theme.
Preach, Queen! waited until he had everyone's full attention again.
When we tell our stories, he continued. When we pass on our folktales and
proverbs and parables that been passed to us by mouth.
We theorize the flesh.
When we trickster our way out this daily nonsense, we theorize.
We theorize, y'all know what we do.
We *make* us, *make* us, some words.
When these don't suit us, don't express what going on, we keep it fresh.
Keep it live.
Because, truth be told, we prefer the dynamic to the fixed.
How else we survived all this?
All this abuse—
There was a chorus.
All this brutality—
You already know—
All this murdered and shot down and worked to death—
What been *done* to our bodies—Preach, Queen! answered the chorus.
To the many ways we define them.
To how we know them.
Our own and differing black bodies—
And then Preach, Queen! paused.
He took a long slow gaze at the faces around the bar.
They were expectant, ready now.
He leapt off his stool.
Onto the bar's top.
He pranced between the glasses and ashtrays underfoot.

Theme's mouth fell open at the spectacular sight of him.

The stubs that were her blue-black dreadlocks trembled with excitement.

Am I not beauty? Preach, Queen! intoned. Am I not beauty in this sweet black dress?

He let more tears flow.

Yes, you is!

Am I not beauty in these thigh-high black boots?

Boy please, Overness felt the lecture, like a sermon, heating in her body.

Am I not theory in the flesh?

With my indigo-tipped fingers and my blue lipstick?

We see you, Lawdt, we see you—

I am *my own black*, Preach, Queen! proclaimed atop the bar.

He stopped in front of Theme.

Bent his long self, slow and low and into her face.

His lips vibrated a breath away from hers.

Everybody up in here is theory in the flesh, hunty, he said to her and snapped his fingers.

And what was human in the bar was suddenly peacock and flamingo.

After a moment, though, they all turned back to human.

Preach, Queen! slipped off the bar and went back to his stool.

As the room filled with hoots and laughter and raucous applause.

Preach, Queen! raised his glass to his students.

He blew them kisses as he twirled about.

He'd taught and he'd been seen.

In here, in this other universe, critical love was a complex possible

From that day forward, Theme was a regular at The Fabulous.

And because of the flamboyant philosopher, she learned to live in her body the way she did.

Neither binary nor reconstructed.

What was the word for hybrid?

Or nature's desire for difference.

For particularity.

Because nature desires the impermissible.

And abhors the prescriptive.

So, at Preach, Queen!'s elbow, Theme learned to theorize desire was the only gender.

And blackness itself was genitalia.

To be pleasured and revered.

Alone and with.

And referring to the self as *we* was more acceptable to the historical soul than the designation *I*

When the detective tucked her notebook and pen away and said finally, We'll take the case, the Nigerian Woman breathed a loud sigh of relief.

Fhill breathed aroused.

But to Fhill's dismay, Theme said, And we'll start today.

Then Theme's eyes went cool, to Fhill.

The sultry light in them absent that had been there that very morning

You sleep, sugah pussy? Theme had said behind her in the bed.

Yeah, Fhill said.

You wanna wake up?

What for, Fhill said.

Theme's breasts poked Fhill's back.

And she grabbed Fhill's hand to bring it backwards.

Squeezed it tight around her dick.

Slowly fucked Fhill's hand.

As Fhill turned onto her belly, arched and submissive.

She'd come to like how Theme fucked.

Like an addictive drug, the fuck was brutal and sweet.

Sex was a language, not just behavior

Theme slapped Fhill's ass.

You like that?

Theme slapped it harder. You like that, sugah pussy?

Fhill whimpered when Theme slapped her ass again.

Then licked it.

Then thrust her dick, hard and shuddering, into Fhill.

As Fhill let out a sharp, wounded cry.

They fucked quick and greedy.
And came sweaty, exhausted.
Theme's blue-black dreads, tumescent.
Theme on Fhill's back.
Shit, girl, Theme said afterwards.
Sleep was the only lubrication

Now, Fhill gazed at Theme out the corner of her eye.
Theme's dreadlocks wriggled blue and black, like antennae.
Stimulated by the private detective's curiosity on the ready.
They sensed Fhill's gaze and bent away from it at once.
A clear sign, Fhill thought, that Theme had a different obsession right then.
Fhill felt a spasm of jealous

All that first day and all that first night, all Aguta and Fhill and Theme talked
about was the disappearance of Oya.
On the second day, Theme disappeared, too.
She's chasing the case, Fhill told herself.
Though that night she felt her need for the detective rise on Aguta's porch

Fhill listened to the Nigerian Woman sing in his rocking chair.
To Preach, Queen!, who rocked in his arms.
Aguta's airy falsetto was solace.
It pricked the scab of grieving for.
His mother had recently crossed over.
And Preach, Queen! was broken.
Like other men, he knew to come to Aguta.
For a reading of the cards.
For counsel.
A tea to calm.
And like the others, Preach, Queen! knew that the embrace of this fathermother
would re-tailor the masculinity he wore

On the second night of the second week, Theme reappeared.
As if no time had passed.

She had a bag full of crab and crawfish and bottles of wine.

Though she had nothing significant to report, she distracted Aguta and Fhill with stories of the fantastic cases she'd solved.

They were at the kitchen table and on their last bottle of wine when Fhill said, This Oya thing damn sure is a puzzle.

To which Theme said, All puzzles can be solved.

But Aguta countered, "Nothing puzzles God," said my good friend Mr. Achebe.[21]

Who, though dead as a man now, Mr. Chinua Achebe flew into Aguta's half shuttered kitchen window as a snowy egret.

He landed on the table.

Looked about at the three of them.

Then Mr. Achebe said:

I was a wordsmith in that life.

Books were my magic.

But I had only imagined God.

I know better now, for I have lived in God.

There is God, my friends, and there is what we in our where know
is More Than God.

Whaaat?! Aguta exclaimed.

Aguta believed in God, but what was this bird talking, More Than God?

Was More Than God just some cockeyed theory of a manbird?

Could God be known through some poetic articulation of embodied experience?

If that were the case, was reality really a legitimate source of Divine revelation?

Are the Divine and the real irreducibly mysterious?

Or are they, like this manbird here, simply metaphors?

What was Oya, for that matter?

For all I know, the Nigerian Woman reasoned to herself, God might be something astral, something separate from the physical and capable of traveling outside the physical throughout the universe.

Only the tortoise knows, Mr. Achebe said, what is hidden in its shell. Let me have sum a dat red bean and rice, sum a dat seafood.

Well, of course Aguta jumped right up and fixed that bird a plate.

---

21 Chinua Achebe, "Civil Peace," in *African Short Stories: Twenty Short Stories from Across the Continent*, eds., Chinua Achebe and C. L. Innes (Oxford: Harcourt, 1985), 34.

Because the ancestors are our living responsibility.

No matter who they belong to, they must be fed.

So, the three of them watched as the snowy egret feasted.

Then, with a belly full and not another word, Mr. Chinua Achebe left the way he came

That night was the last Fhill spent with Theme as time went by.

To keep herself busy she worked extra kitchen shifts at the school and took longer walks with Nommo by the river in the evenings.

She longed for that sweet hurt.

But Theme was in pursuit of a puzzle.

So Theme scoured the neighborhoods of the city.

Day and night.

Still, no one had seen Oya.

Though that was not unusual, for Oya was tiny indeed.

And thus, was not often seen by most humans when she was about.

For the humans thought it beneath themselves to look down

With each passing day, the return of the mysterious Oya seemed hopeless to the Nigerian Woman.

But her private detective, her private dick it amused Aguta to say, pressed on.

Firm in the belief that mystery was kin to miracle

Late one night, as Theme exited The Fabulous, the streetcar juggling down Canal, passed by.

And there, in the back row, looking out the window at Theme was the Nigerian Woman's Oya.

Perched atop the headrest of a seat.

Oya gave Theme a mischievous grin as she went by.

A strong sudden wind blew Theme off balance.

And she stumbled, as she'd had more than one whiskey that night.

By the time she recovered her composure, the green streetcar with its red doors had vanished.

Even so, the private detective rushed to her client's house across town

Aguta and Fhill were sitting on the porch.

In the sticky night's quiet, they sipped hot tea to cool themselves off.

When Theme rushed onto the porch and shouted,

I have seen Oya!

Aguta leapt up. Praise God, you have found her!

I have not found her, Theme said.

But you just said—Fhill said.

I have seen her, Theme said.

The Nigerian Woman squinted with suspicion. How do you know that
what you have seen is my Oya?

Because, the detective giggled and her dreadlocks bent inappropriately, I know
a clue when I see one.

And with that, Theme Le Roy teetered off the porch.

She wobbled down the night-thick street.

Aguta and Fhill watched her go.

Too stunned to say anything, they went back to their tea.

And though the streetcar was long gone, to Theme the scent of mysterious was
not

So strong was the scent the next day that Theme easily found and followed Oya
as she traveled the city.

Close though out of sight, the detective tailed her discreetly.

First, Oya hopped the streetcar up St. Charles, to the park.

Where she sat on a bench by the bayou.

Chatted with the ducks and swans.

As the herbivores complained: The humans throw us old bread for food.
We prefer plants.

As I do, Oya commiserated.

When she had heard as much as she could stand of the situation, Oya helped
the herbivores come up with a plan.

And they all waited for the next group of humans to saunter by.

When the humans threw the old bread, this time the herbivores
threw it back.

Which sent the confused and irate humans scurrying away.

Muttering about the arrival of the alien.

It was just frightening, they said to each other, the way the earth
and the bayou... and the creatures in their eyes...
Satisfied with the way things had turned out, Oya bid the ducks and swans
good luck and goodbye.
Once outside the park, she took a leisurely stroll down Magazine Street and
stopped at a café.
When she'd eaten all the okra stew she could, she went on her way.
Unbeknownst to the crafty detective, Oya was well aware that Theme was fol-
lowing her.
Across town, Oya stopped on Basin Street.
Where she entered the gate to Cemetery No. 1

In the cemetery, Theme ducked out of sight.
As Oya led the unsuspecting detective through a labyrinth of above-ground
vaults.
The veil in the seam of what was, is, and will be, thin, within and between them.
At last, Oya stopped at the Vault of Marie-Marie.
Who'd once lived as god-human in this city.
She died, it was said, of natural causes, but no one could ever explain
how natural happened to the supernatural.
As the tale goes, though, Marie-Marie lived a magical life on Earth until
the day she was seen among the humans no more.
But she lived on.
As Oya knew.
The desires of the Divine were incongruous with finite realities.
So, Oya sat beside the vault, aware of the snooping detective

After a while, Theme Le Roy approached the spot where Oya sat.
Why have you run away?
I have not run away, Oya said. I am concealed.
Your Aguta is a devoted follower, Theme said.
Oya bristled.
And a strong sudden gust blew.
Theme maintained her balance.
I cannot be what I am solely in a corner, Oya said.

Since it appears you are in no hurry to return, what shall we do? Theme said.

The devotee cannot dictate the arc of the poet, Oya said.

And so, Theme left the cemetery and boarded the streetcar

On the way to Aguta's house, she decided to reward herself first.

She jumped off just as the streetcar approached The Fabulous.

By the time she and Preach, Queen! left the bar and went their separate ways,
the moon was half asleep.

In its light, Theme's skin turned bluest.

And she shown against the night's own blue like a shadow and the whites of its
Eyes

The Nigerian Woman was elated by Theme's news.

But he was confused.

What did it mean that Oya was concealed?

The detective contemplated the Nigerian Woman's question.

And then, in the quiet of Aguta's candle-filled living room, Theme said:

We have arrived at the conclusion of our investigation.

And we have deduced the following.

Oya is not a statue.

Though she sometimes appears that way.

She is a god of transformation from one state of being to another.

She can be wind and she can be solid.

She has the power to perform effective magic.

She concealed herself so that she could be seen—

Yes, yes. Yes, of course, Aguta let his agitation loose.

Then let the current settle between them before Theme continued:

Oya is significant to the material and nonmaterial realms of being human.

As would be any revolutionary. Trust me.

She must live here as fully as you.

She cannot be excluded from the cult and culture of your men.

And having revealed all that she'd conjured about the slippery nature of facts,
Theme Le Roy placed a white envelope with her bill inside on Aguta's coffee ta-
ble.

Good night, she said. Then left.

One morning several days later, the Nigerian Woman went out on his porch to greet the day.

He found Oya there.

Rocking in his singing chair.

The sight of Oya startled Aguta, but he remembered what the private detective had said.

So, the Nigerian Woman gathered her kaftan about himself with a flourish.

He sat in the other chair.

Sipped his tea as New Orleans awoke to another sticky day

Theme Le Roy took on a case almost immediately after solving that one.

She went out of town and Fhill did not see Theme after that.

The absence hurt as much as the longing.

That was the thing about pleasure's magic.

You could be addicted.

With it.

Or without it

INTER**SPECIES**

They did not speak the same way.

They did, however, talk.

With looks, stares, they gave each other.

They'd lived as such, each learning the other, for the better part of several years.

They were companions.

Any other word for what they shared would unleash

the stench of the proprietary

Fhill was thinking that as she side-stepped Nommo outside her bedroom door.

There was a splash of water on the floor coming from the bathroom.

Nommo saw her see it.

Then he casually looked away, seeing something she did not.

Good morning, Fhill said. Hungry?

Nommo's look told her, as it always did, the rhetorical had no meaning.

And she let out a soft chuckle.

As they made their way downstairs.

Quietly tiptoeing.

As one.

They'd lived closely for so long it was hard, sometimes, to tell when the canine was not human and the human not canine

On the first floor of their home, spears of light hummed through the shutters.

Cascaded over the dark, well-polished wood floors.

The light shadowed the window seat in the foyer.

Fhill could see that the hibiscus and ficus and arugula cohabitating in pots in the living and sitting rooms were erect, awakening to the morning.

Nommo moseyed over to them.

She carefully sniffed each one, ferreting out the scent of growth night deposited.

Fhill collected the wine glasses and juice bottles from the coffee table.

And then, as did Nommo, followed a scent into the kitchen

Emma sat at the table.
Her black notebook open.
The poem she was writing, in her eyes.
Her hands cupped a mason jar of fresh-brewed black coffee.
She managed a thin smile when Nommo came and sat beside her.
The dog was nice enough, but.
It wasn't clear *what* Nommo was.
Why his tail and left hind leg was black.
Why he was missing a toe on that black paw.
Why the rest of him was bleach white.
The dog had a penis and full breasts

In the city's Harbor Park, Fhill walked down by the river.
It was her day off.
The look of the day was maudlin.
The weather upstate was just turning cold.
The usually boisterous seagulls nested at the pier.
Fhill spotted the lump beneath a bench.
As she approached it, she could see the dog.
Closer, she could see the litter of dead pups.
The dog stared at her a while.
Then it looked at the huddled dead one last time.
The dog followed Fhill the whole walk home

The Art of the Dogon was the title of a book she'd found in a closet her first
week in the house.
She'd discovered, flipping through it, the Nommo were believed to be water
spirits

How'd you sleep? Fhill took the carton of half and half out of the refrigerator.
Nommo watched, intently.
Emma yawned. Not too well. She massaged her protruding belly.
This one is a night owl, she said.
Like father like daughter, Fhill said.
She poured some coffee and some half and half into a tin bowl.

Before she could put the bowl down on the floor, Nommo was in his spot.

In three quick slurps, the bowl was empty.

And Nommo swiped his whiskers with a long, pink tongue.

Emma yawned again.

I'm happy for Fawnie, she said. Having a sister means a lot—

You taught me that, Fhill said.

What we've taught each other, Emma said.

Fhill grinned, poured herself some coffee, and sat at the table.

She sipped from the mermaid-shaped mug while Emma jotted something in her notebook

Nommo marched out of the kitchen.

As if someone, or something, had called.

Went upstairs.

Went into the bathroom.

Jumped over the lip of the tub.

In the just-enough water, Nommo happily splashed, doing his ritual.

He was on his back, panting into a furious kick when his ears lifted.

Emma stood in the bathroom doorway.

She watched him, with a scowl meant to punish.

He just looked at her.

Like she had lost her mind, she felt.

He waited.

His legs, suspended in the air.

Emma was baffled.

Why was this dog in the tub again?

What possessed the dog to bathe, if that was what he was doing, where she and her six-year-old washed naked.

How did this dog get water in the tub?

Fhill had to know.

Fhill had to know what the dog did in her bathroom.

But why did she allow it.

Why didn't this fucking dog stay in its own lane?

Momma? Fawn came up behind Emma.

The freckles swam across her nose.

Her doe-y curls tossed by dream.

She rubbed sleep from her eyes.

I gotta wee wee, Fawn said.

Emma glanced over at Nommo.

So still the dog was, practically invisible.

O sure, baby, Emma said to Fawn.

Then glanced at the statue dog.

Fawn pulled at her pajama bottoms and wiggled them to her ankles.

She scooted over to the toilet.

Stopped and blinked at the sight of Nommo.

Momma, why she froze like that?

Nommo likes to play hide-and-seek. Pretend like you don't see him.

She gonna be in the tub with me? Fawn sat on the toilet.

Let's skip the bath today, Emma said. Just wash your hands and face.

And brush your teeth baby, hurry up.

A bowl of granola and blueberries and a tall glass of milk waited for Fawn in the kitchen.

Fhill emptied the dishwasher.

As Emma came in holding Fawn's pawish hand.

Good morning, Fawnie, Fhill said. We got you your favorite breakfast.

She nodded at the blue cereal bowl.

Good morning, Goddess Mother, Fawn said, wide eyed. Sat down.

Your dog is in the bathtub, Emma droned.

Uh huh, Fhill said. Thought: Canine.

She put away the silverware.

Don't you wonder about him, even a little? Emma said.

Nope.

Didn't you tell me you've seen him—Emma glanced at Fawn, then spelled out—f-u-c-k-i-n the neighbor's dog, Ringo?

Yep. Fhill put away some pots and pans.

And wasn't it their other dog, Lilly Pad, who was doing it to him?

Fhill shot Emma a look. So?

So, he goes both ways, Emma said.

She *is* both ways, Fhill said.
Well, there's different and then there's different, Emma said.
Don't you love Lune? Fhill said. Ain't Lune different?

And what could Emma say but that look.
You'd have to be blind not to see.
Lune had whiskers where another had a mustache.
He was feline.
He made his living hunting and killing rats for the city's overwrought restaurant owners.
Much to Emma's amazement, he perched atop the refrigerator to eat tuna out the can.
When he was satisfied, he purred.
He insisted she call him Big Pussy when he made love to her.
It made him hard.
Made his lovemaking wild.
Emma'd known for some time.
She was living with a hybrid

Nommo padded down the back stairs.
She stopped at the bottom and shook water from her fur.
Then she gave Emma side-eye as she went out his door and into the patchy green backyard

In humans, it is said, the spirit lived in the body, unseen and unseeable.
Dependent and wedded, throughout the life of the body, to the body.
But Nommo's spirit ÷ from Nommo's body when it wanted to, because it lived on its own.
Because every species has a talent.
And every living thing hungers to be seen.
Which made it possible for Nommo to be in a here and in an otherwhere at the same time.
In the backyard, Nommo's spirit took off

Fhill wiped up Nommo's wet tracks and finished tidying the kitchen.

She reminded herself what day it was.

For Nommo and her kind.

Beast Valley—as the humans called it—was for canine wilding out.

Once a year, the city's officials encouraged "dog owners" to bring their "pets."

To mingle with the canines who live there without leashes, sit commands, or human rule.

As Fhill watched Nommo from the kitchen window.

Just standing in the yard, looking at something she could not see.

Fhill was sure Nommo knew today was the day

Nommo was sitting upright in the back seat of the Cadillac convertible, waiting.

When Fhill and Emma and Fawn finally emerged from the house.

Emma looked at the dog.

She shook her head in resignation.

This just didn't match.

This together way they lived.

It did not match Fhill's tales of having grown up in a neglected neighborhood in the South Bronx.

Where mangy dogs terrorized the residents night and day.

They mauled garbage cans, she'd said, in search of food.

If humans got too close, they'd bare their teeth.

They'd foam at the mouth, she'd said, she was petrified at the sight of a dog.

She'd run into the nearest storefront, the nearest building.

Sweating fear.

How many times had Fhill said to her, Baby I hate dogs

Emma hoisted Fawn into the spacious seat beside Nommo.

She watched Fhill round the wide front of the car.

Her breasts full under her clothes.

The way her pelvis rolled as she walked.

Her keys in her hand.

The easy way of charisma

She was later than she'd planned to be, though she loved making an entrance.

Emma slinked through the apartment full of women perfuming the air.

The form-fitting black sheath she wore highlighted her curvy frame, in fact.

A woman approached her.

Staring down at her feet.

I like your shoes, the woman said.

Thank you, Emma said.

Are they Tookie Smith's?

Emma's eyes locked on the dandyish woman. I'm impressed, she said.

So am I, the woman said. You pamper your feet. I'm Fhill.

Emma, Emma said.

You know anybody here?

Aurora and Hamp, Emma said. They always throw a good party.

Fhill took a swig of her beer. I like your feet, she said into her bottle

Now, of course, there is no such love as heaven.

In brief time, they each felt the sweet go.

So, they went from being lovers to fondly friends

Emma got in the front seat.

Fhill guided the tank of a car out of the driveway.

Emma noted that it was still spotless.

Still smelled of new car leather.

Fhill's Cadillac still had those white wall tires.

Out of the city the two-door silver blue convertible truly looked much happier.

You know what, Goddess Mother? Fawn said from the back seat.

What baby?

Nommo is licking my leg. And before, she was licking my face.

Fhill glanced at her goddaughter in the rearview mirror.

That's how he kisses people he likes, she said.

Isn't this fun? Emma said.

No matter what, it was good to see Fhill.

It'd been too long.

They'd always have what they'd always had.

She could feel it.

Emma threaded her fingers through Fhill's free hand.

And when Fhill gave them a gentle squeeze, Emma settled into the ride out to

Beast Valley

The breeze washed Nommo's face, and he greeted its insistent touch sticking his nose into it.

He looked about.

To everyone else in the car, he was enjoying the ride.

But part of him, the ÷ part, was already where they had yet to come.

That part went into the bushes of Beast Valley.

And stopped in a corridor of trees.

A humanoid in a dark hoodie peeled off the ground.

Luminescent.

It shimmered, like a hologram.

And though it was three dimensional, the Ever All violated logic as it hovered slightly above the ground.

It was an astral rapture, the Ecstatic Word, originating in the answer to a question:

What more,

and more precisely

what else,

what else was there

of life,

of its forms,

its hybridities?

The figure walked toward Nommo.

When they were only a few feet apart, Nommo bent his head in deference.

The figure came close.

Nommo collapsed onto her back.

She let the shimmering figure rub her belly vigorously.

The humanoid got down on all fours.

Then the two nuzzled and pawed each other, admiring one another.

And sat, side by side, looking at what only they could see.

Their thoughts and feelings bleeding through epidermis for what did not feel like, but was, a long time

The area where the humans parked their cars was on a hill.
From there the full vista of Beast Valley was visible:
It was a tract of land outside the city proper.
The prehistoric, densely spaced trees were matted together in families.
Their towering necks bent at the top, competing for shits of sunlight.
They communicated, through electrical impulses and their own senses
of smell and taste.
The ground beneath them was choked with bulbous, crawling roots.
An umbrella of smaller trees weaved beneath the taller ones.
They nurtured the stump of a felled tree, feeding it sugars and other nutrients.
Even without a breeze everything was in motion, preening, adrenalized

The canines were not visible at first.
But then the prehistoric green began to mutate.
And there they were: tails wagging, roaming about in tribes.
Standing still.
Staring up at the humans on the hill.
Though Beast Valley had been designated by the city's humans as "a dog park,"
humans were neither in control nor welcome within it.
In fact, it was the canines who'd chosen this place to be.
Nommo bolted from the back seat.
He tore down the embankment, along with several others.
The newcomers let their butts be sniffed.
Until what was to be known about their diets, genders, their emotional states—
written in the biographies of sharp odor and pheromones—was known to the
waiting pack

Emma let Fawn out of the car.
She squinted at the scene below.
I see what you mean, she said to Fhill.
Yeah, it's pretty wild, Fhill admitted.
Inhospitable, Emma countered. I wouldn't call this place an enchanted forest.
People say, Fhill said, there's something in there. That can change humans into
dogs.
Emma sucked her teeth in loud disbelief. Gurl, please.

Fhill chuckled. Come on, Fawnie, let's get a balloon.

And with that, Fhill took Fawn's hand and started for the concession area

At a nearby table, a city employee, with the name tag Huber, announced the city's animal rescue hotline with a pile of brochures and free buttons.

Huber hovered between long ears, dog paws, and an elongated, hound dog nose.

Huber wore baggy jeans and an oversized t-shirt.

And scratched, from time to time, with one paw furiously.

The city employee was accompanied by a teenaged human who handed out balloons.

He handed Fawn a blue-and-green balloon on a long string.

The balloon resembled planet Earth

Emma came up behind them.

Well, that's stupid. Fhill frowned.

What? Emma said.

Hot dogs. Fhill pointed at the lone food truck. Why would they have hot dogs, of all things to eat, here?

Emma regarded the truck. Animal behavior, she said, animal behavior and other human activities.

Yeah, Fhill grunted, let's sit down.

A few feet away, Emma and Fhill settled onto an unoccupied bench under a tree.

Fawn hovered off to the side.

She gazed transfixed as a tiny girl consumed an enormous hot dog.

A blob of yellow mustard dirtied the girl's otherwise pristine white dress.

As the girl swiped at the stain, she looked to see if anyone was watching.

She stuck out her tongue at Fawn.

It was littered with half-chewed bun and meat.

The sight made Fawn blink.

Irritated, the little girl stomped off.

And Fawn stuck out her tongue at the girl's back.

A flirty breeze whipped the balloon about.

Emma surveyed the thin crowd at the food truck.

She watched a woman in line ignore the insistent chihuahua who humped the woman's leg.

Animals did what they wanted.

Clearly.

Upstate, people were just as wild as their creatures.

Anything was possible, Emma thought.

She gave Fhill a quick onceover.

There was something different.

She sensed it.

Sure as someone without sight sensed light.

I never thought you'd be out of the city this long, she said to Fhill. You must like it—

Too much drama in the city, Fhill said. Turned to look at Fawn wandering around behind them.

Fawn talked to her balloon.

What happened to you? Emma said.

All the feet started to look the same. Fhill studied the thin black leather straps of the sandals across Emma's thick toes.

The manicured toes lay atop one another, polished black.

The bunions on the sides of her feet swelled outward.

A stunted sixth toe on her left foot had changed its mind about coming out mature.

That married woman still seeing you? Emma said.

Fhill's laugh was from surprised. Why? You jealous?

Emma brushed a lick of red curls from her face.

Then massaged her belly.

Laughed too. Maybe, she said.

A squat, sweating woman deposited herself at the other end of their bench.

She held tight to the leash of the large black and gray German shepherd attached to a choke collar.

The dog's tail dripped between his hind legs.

He waited until the woman looked at him before he sat down.

Fhill eyed the German shepherd and the woman he was with.

There was no mistaking.

He lived by her rule.

He had a place in her home because he was obedient.

He ate good at her expense.

She expected him to protect her.

Here, and everywhere.

She was the alpha dog

Nommo appeared on the periphery of the embankment.

She sat on his haunches.

Glanced back over his left shoulder.

She looked at the Ever All shimmering inside its hoodie.

When Fhill spotted Nommo, she wondered what Nommo was looking at

The early spring wind belched around them.

Fawn squealed as her balloon became kite.

The woman felt pinched by the child's sound.

Get that thing out of my face, she barked.

And slapped Fawn's kite away from her.

Fawn ran into her mother's arms.

Hey! What's your problem? Fhill addressed the woman.

For Christ's sake, Emma said, it's a fucking balloon—

The woman sprang up, wound tight.

The world was scary without her Jimmy.

Jimmy had loved and protected her for forty-two years.

He'd understood she was nervous by nature.

Change was hard for her.

When no one else did, he'd understood she needed a rock.

Jimmy had been her Lollipop and she, his Plum Pie.

Now, all she had was his walking buddy, Pal.

Was company enough, but no dog, nothing, could replace her Jimmy.

Gone to glory, bless him.

What was she to do?

She snarled even louder. I said keep it away from me!

Nommo crouched forward, with the humanoid beside him, stalking the woman.

He let out a low, rattled growl.

Fhill stood up just then.

She towered over the squat woman shaking visibly.

Look, lady, Fhill said, you need to calm the hell down—

The woman jerked tighter the choke collar around Pal's neck.

The pinch of it momentarily strangled.

She shook violently now.

You don't tell me what to do.

You, you, you,

you nigger!

And right then, the hooded figure hovering beside Nommo, the figure only Nommo could see, brightened in frequency.

And Fhill sprung forward with vicious speed.

As canine and incisor, as premolar teeth flashed.

Fhill's bite slit the woman's mouth.

What the—! Emma said, startled.

She and Fawn stood at Fhill's back.

Emma kept one eye on the few people watching.

The woman backed away from Fhill.

Though she tried, she could not speak.

But she tasted the fact:

Fhill had spit in her mouth

You okay? Emma said. Still baffled by what she'd seen.

Goddess Mother? Fawn said.

I'm fine baby, Fhill said. Glaring at the woman as she pulled her dog toward the parking area.

It wasn't clear now which one of them was on the leash.

Nothing's changed, Emma said.

She has, Fhill said. She'll watch her mouth from now on

Nommo walked up to them. She gave Fhill a tender look. Then she sat down, lifted that left hind leg, and licked herself.

And the space of the missing toe of that black paw.

When she was finished, she looked over her left shoulder.
To see the humanoid headed into the dense bush, its light less intense.
Nommo headed for the car

That night, after Fawn was asleep, Emma headed for Fhill's bedroom.
And later, when all the humans were snoring at last, Nommo went out her door
and into the backyard and collected her spirit.
And then went through the gate, past the convertible sleeping in the driveway,
and down the street's deserted black

CITY OF PARABLES

Miss Nana had a snake in her belly.

Snake, people said.

It was alcoholic.

Plus, she had the sugah.

So, the doctors cut her toes then her feet off.

Which meant she never left the house.

That day, she was sitting in her spot at her apartment window.

When the two teenagers turned the corner

Miss Nana called out, Yoohoo!

Fhill looked up at the third-floor corner window.

A white handkerchief waved in Miss Nana's hand.

Hey, Miss Nana, Whiskey said.

Whatchu want? Fhill hollered up.

You know what she want, Whiskey said.

Fhill sucked her teeth.

Why couldn't this ma get somebody else to run her errand.

There was plenty of other kids around.

They'd gladly take her money for a few minutes of run up and down.

She always caught the two of them, though.

There was a consequence for that.

Delivery price gone up, Fhill shouted.

That's fine. Miss Nana grinned.

Disappeared inside

Fhill and Whiskey went up to Miss Nana's apartment.

When they got to Miss Nana's floor, Fhill stopped.

What? Whiskey said.

You know I wanted to do something else now, Fhill said.

We got plenty of time for that. We help Miss Nana, she help us get some herb, right?

Fhill rubbed Whiskey's bald head. You so smart.

Miss Nana was in the curtained living room when Fhill and Whiskey came in.
Her face was a flawless mask of blue powder, blue lipstick, and long false eye-
lashes.
She leaned on the frayed couch.
Propped up on the two kneepads that functioned as feet.
Miss Nana stuck out a handful of balled-up bills.
Which Fhill took immediately.
Handed over to Whiskey to count

Make sure Jack Rabbit give me a big bottle, Miss Nana said.
Scrutinized the two teenagers.
She could trust them, she knew.
All these two ever wanted was the money.
They'd get what they wanted.
And she'd get some relief from the parasitic twitching inside her.
The snake under Miss Nana's house dress visibly moved.
Fhill and Whiskey watched the bubble of it but said nothing.
All their lives the adults on the block had one rule: Stay out grown folks' business

Be right back, Whiskey said.
Then nudged Fhill out the apartment door.
Down on the first floor they turned under the stairs and through the unlocked
door that led to the basement.
It always stank.
Mountains of busted toilets.
With the insides leaking from ragged upholstered chairs.
In the basement's dark, things moved and whispered and changed form.
Like haints, with nothing painted that blue to ward them off.
Fhill felt uneasy, jittery.
She pushed Whiskey ahead of her toward the wall with the missing bricks

After a moment, Jack Rabbit's hand extended out.
Her long, blue-tipped fingers wiggled.
Until Whiskey placed Miss Nana's money in Jack Rabbit's palm.
Miss Nana want a big bottle, Whiskey said. Please.

And hurry up, Fhill said under her breath.
Jack Rabbit's fingers moved, to see the money and count it.
Then closed tight around the bills.
The hand retreated

When the bottle of moonshine finally slid out of the hole, Fhill snatched it quick.
Grabbed Whiskey's hand and bolted from the basement.
Once they were safely on the first floor, she opened the jug and took
a sip to calm her nerves.
Back in Miss Nana's apartment, Fhill collected their delivery tip before turning
over the moonshine

And right then, because she was feeling cocky.
Because she wanted satisfaction and not rules, Fhill said.
That really a snake in your belly?
O snap, Whiskey said, let's go.
Nawww, Fhill said. I wanna know. I wanna know what that thing is—
Miss Nana's eyes glazed over

As was their custom, Nana and her girlfriend, Lane, met every month at Plea-
sure, Aurora Pierce's beauty parlor.
A neighborhood establishment, Pleasure specialized in Aurora's flower philoso-
phy, catering to collective blooming rather than individual beauty.
Aurora believed beauty multiplied beauty.
And that it was a shame not to be reflected.
In order to be serviced at her shop, you had to bring family or lover or friend with
you, no matter the genders

Once, after they'd each gotten their hair done, Nana and Lane sat side by side
waiting for a pedicure.
When it was their turn, Lane took a naughty stroll over to Constance's chair.
And Nana slid into Hamp's.
Hamp was Aurora's husband.
A handsome, debonair woman.
She flirted with the clients, and she dripped charm.

How you doing today, beautiful? Hamp winked at Nana.

I'm fine, Nana giggled.

All right then, Hamp said. Then re-rolled her shirt sleeves and flipped her tie over a shoulder.

Gently placed Nana's feet in the turn of warm, gurgling water.

As Nana settled into Hamp's chair.

And Hamp hummed to her toes and kneaded Nana's soles.

And before she dozed off to sleep, Nana noticed that Constance, Lane's sweet thing, was rubbing Lane's feet but staring at her.

Hard

Knowing something can be the beginning of the end of you, Miss Nana said to Fhill.

Fhill swaggered into the moment. You tryna scare me ma?

Miss Nana's snake beat against her insides with a furious thirst.

She guzzled half the bottle of moonshine.

Wincing as she did so.

The alcohol was the only thing that quieted the pain.

Whenever she made Snake wait for it though, even a minute too long, Snake punished her with its coil and recoil and diagonal twitching

Miss Nana sat back on her legs.

She was matter-of-fact. You really want to know?

Too many years had gone by to hold onto shame, she'd told herself.

At some point, you have to admit you live with demons.

Once upon a time, I laid with another woman's husband, Miss Nana said. The woman was a friend of mine.

Fhill sneered. Your friend?

Good friend, Miss Nana said. I just wanted a taste. A taste of that Constance.

But Lane found out.

So, you was a homewrecker—Fhill's laugh was mean.

Did she leave that cheater? Whiskey said.

She went to VooDoo, Miss Nana said.

Then rubbed her belly.

It was quiet. Snake was tipsy in there now.

I'd a left that fool, Whiskey said.

One night at that Fabulous bar, VooDoo put something in my drink.

Fhill's eyes went wide. VooDoo put something in your drink?

Put this snake in my belly. Fixed me. But gave Lane justice, Miss Nana reported.

So, Whiskey said, you can't get ridder the fix?

If I wanted it off, it woulda passed to Constance's little girl. And I couldn't see doing that.

You know what? Fhill said. This sound like something you made up.

And I don't believe a word of it.

Fhill turned to Whiskey. Come on let's go—

Bye Miss Nana, Whiskey said.

Have fun, Miss Nana said, be careful.

Sometime later, Whiskey noticed that Fhill was skipping school.

Right when it was their last months before high school graduation.

She wasn't on the block.

And nobody knew where she was.

Until the day Whiskey spotted Fhill grinning behind the wheel of Aurora Pierce's two-door silver blue Cadillac convertible.

Driving down the street like it was hers.

With Aurora beside her in the front seat.

Aurora was a woman practiced in taking care of herself.

She was a pretty, manicured, black.

She sold beauty because she knew what beauty do.

And what it craved.

The Cadillac slithered up to the curb

Where you been? Whiskey spoke to Fhill. Eyed the older woman.

On the road, Fhill said.

On the road? What road?

That ain't none a your business, Fhill said.

But what about the prom?

Probably ain't going. Fhill turned from Whiskey's startled look.

But what about me? Whiskey pleaded.

What about you? Aurora Pierce swallowed the trembling girl with an eye.

She reapplied her white lipstick in the car's interior mirror.

Inspected her dusky face.

Then motioned Fhill to drive on.

Fhill grinned and pulled the car away with a cocky finesse.

Whiskey put her hand on her hip and snapped.

God don't like ugly, and little do she care for beauty, she screamed.

One afternoon, as Hamp drove to New Jersey to pick up an order from a wholesale beauty supplier, Aurora lay in their bed with Fhill.

The sex was sweet.

And the girl eager to please that day but.

You tired? Fhill said.

No baby, Aurora said.

So, what's wrong?

Nothing honey, Aurora said.

Something's wrong, Fhill said. You not really here. I can tell.

I just wish my husband had eyes only for me, Aurora said.

Yeah. Fhill sneered. I seen the way Hamp be looking. All the women want him and all the men want to be him.

But me myself, I don't see nobody but you.

So, you don't need that fool.

Well, it didn't take long.

Because Hamp Pierce was no fool.

He lived by the street's code.

What belonged to him, belonged to him only.

That Aurora, that fine black confection, that was his.

So, one night, when Aurora paraded Fhill around the bar at The Fabulous,

Hamp Pierce, the gentleman that she was, bought her woman and that young trick a round of drinks.

And when nobody was watching, Hamp slipped justice into Fhill's drink

Two days later, Fhill woke up in Aurora's bed.

She was alone.

She went from room to room in the apartment.

As empty as a new rental.

There was no sign of Aurora.

Or Hamp.

On her way out, she saw the image of herself in the hallway mirror.

She had a frog's head.

With two bulbous red eyes on either side of her frog face

Fhill's mother took Fhill from one doctor to another.

The doctors shook their heads in disbelief.

Nothing could be done.

So Fhill stayed home and did not leave the house.

Until a neighbor told her mother, Take your daughter to VooDoo.

As soon as VooDoo laid eyes on the teenager, VooDoo knew:

She'd made a mistake in judgment.

VooDoo felt sorry for her, the girl was too young to wear life.

But this was a sign.

Evil wasn't simply bad.

Evil lived in an excess of pleasure

Take your daughter home, VooDoo instructed Fhill's mother.

Cook she two egg.

She gone sleep three day.

She wake up the fourth.

Be she self again.

And though nobody but VooDoo knew how, that is exactly what happened

It took a long time for Fhill and Whiskey to be close again.

Though Fhill apologized over and over, Whiskey's heart refused to forget.

The shop of pleasure, closed.

And they never saw or spoke of Aurora Pierce or her husband Hamp.

And though the silver blue Cadillac convertible disappeared too, it stayed se-
cretly in Fhill's heart.

The sight of cooked eggs sickened her.

As did milk and cheese.

She no longer ate her mother's smothered pork chops, bacon for breakfast, or fried chicken.

Some years later, grown and on her own now, and when she considered living with a dog, she happened upon a book at the public library, *What Animals Know.*

Reading it, Fhill discovered that other animals knew humans used them for food and labor.

For novelty and protection.

Animals knew they were sacrificed in the name of belief and human social order. And they were waiting for the day

JOLLY NIGGER BANK

When the day awoke, a spell was cast

To the day's inhabitants it was just rain.
A furious rain.
Water lashed the city's humid, tree-dense streets.
It disappeared distinction between sidewalk and curb.
It whirlpooled from gutters and clogged storm drains.
The rain gave cars water wings as they splashed through the flash flooding.
The storm-weary residents of New Orleans tucked themselves under umbrellas
and resolve.
After all, it wasn't a hurricane.
So, they sighed.
And went out to work.
To the stores.
To borrow from their neighbors the sugar in the salt

It was only rain, so the humans thought.
However stressful it was to move through it, the rain made their lives easier.
It watered their gardens.
And rinsed their streets.
When it rained, their animals were pleasured.
Their own skins glistened from moisture sexed by rain.
From the earthy scent, the petrichor, produced when rain fell on their dry planet.
Yes, to the human beings of this city it was just rain.
But it was also Ever All.
Life that thrived outside of, beyond, their planet.
Ever All was, as one of their scholars had pointed out, an "otherwise
possibility," one of an infinite number of alternatives to what is.[22]

---

22 See Ashon Crawley, *Black Pentecostal Breath: The Aesthetics of Possibility* (New York: Ford-
ham University Press, 2017).

It was shape but had no shape.
The nipple that human life drank its breath from, indeed.
The breath of the Universe.
Ever All.

The rain will stop, Preach, Queen! pleaded over the phone.
Fhill sucked her teeth. Lemme think about it, she said.
I'll come get you. Preach, Queen! hung up.
And before Fhill could turn around, Preach, Queen! was at her door.
He twirled a lily pad of a parasol

By the time they got to the third thrift shop, they hadn't bought anything.
And Fhill was wet and cranky.
But Preach, Queen! was in heaven as she moseyed through the store's neat
chaos.
He salivated over the racks of vintage skirts and dresses.
Amid the marble figurines.
Colorful old dish collections.
Lamps of all sizes spilling everywhere.
Because of a mountain of chairs, one aisle was impassable.
To Fhill, the whole place seemed a humongous mess overwhelming the small
space

A collection of brass candlestick holders and glass bottles parted of their own
accord.
Just as Fhill squeezed past the table they sat on.
And then Fhill saw it, behind them.
The cast iron man-head and torso.
With its exaggerated lips painted red.
That mouth of cruel white teeth and its lascivious, pink tongue.
That negroid that was the nose.
The eyes that consumed the face.
The smiling ridicule undeniable of the caricature

It disgusted her.

And she rattled a frail grandfather clock as she bumped away.

Preach, Queen! came up behind her. What's wrong?

That, Fhill pointed. It's grotesque.

Preach, Queen! picked up the figurine.

The store's owner stepped out from a beaded curtain.

Can I help you?

The proprietor peeked at Fhill and Preach, Queen! through her oversized square-framed eyeglasses.

She walked slowly, perched on kitten heels, towards them.

That jungle of blue-rinsed afro.

The exquisite roundness of face and flawless make up.

Reflected in her waistless body.

Sheathed, as it was, in a stylish checkered suit, marjorelle blue.

Mrs. Overness was old and young in the same breath.

She was impeccable

Give me a coin. Preach, Queen! instructed Fhill.

What? Fhill said.

It's a mechanical bank, Preach, Queen! said. They were quite popular in the 18– and 19-hundreds—

Still were, up till not *that* long ago. If truth be told, Mrs. Overness said.

It was part of a whole material world, the everyday. Preach, Queen! listed: ashtrays, shoe polish, salt and pepper shakers, games, cereal boxes, sheet music, baking powder tins, fishing lures, detergent boxes.

Otherwise known as the visual culture of the race-makers.

All that Topsy and Mammy and Coon, Fhill said.

She remembered then reading *Little Black Sambo*, as a child.

Watching those characters who peopled the "Amos N Andy" series.

In a televised version of her Harlem.

The men, loud, lazy, inept schemers scared of their own shadows.

The women, domineering, aggressive sapphires.

She'd laughed at them.

Back then, she was Judy Garland, Bing Crosby, and Fred Astaire, all in black face in the golden age of the Hollywood musical.

She was Birmingham Brown, the perennially pop-eyed chauffeur of that caricature detective, Charlie Chan (the actor wasn't even Asian).

In the minstrel show.

In the minstrel show that was American life, where her people were envied, a source of fascination, objects of desire.

Feared

Give me a coin! Preach, Queen! urged.

Fhill fished around in her pockets.

My dear husband, Heaven, had a fondness for the belongings of the recently dead, Mrs. Overness volunteered.

She peered at the store's mix of contents. He collected the darnedest things.

Fhill extended a couple of coins, and Preach, Queen! snatched up a penny.

He placed it in the figurine's bent one-armed palm.

Up shot the hand to its mouth.

And as it gobbled the penny, its tongue disappeared and its eyeballs rolled up in its head.

Mrs. Overness muttered, Jim Crow law, Jim Crow etiquette.

So, this was a piggy bank? Fhill said, her initial disgust seduced by fascination.

It was propaganda, Preach, Queen! sneered.

He set the figurine down on the table.

I wonder how long it's been sitting there, Mrs. Overness pondered. We don't usually display this stuff.

She said *we*. Though her husband was long dead, they were still married, she thought.

She kept him like one of the store's treasures, unlike the families of the gone who had unthinkingly thrown what was once love into the archive trash

Mrs. Overness ambled off absent minded.

She ignored Preach, Queen!'s chatter about two fabulous skirts.

At the glass case that was the store's counter, she stopped and turned around.

More focused than she'd appeared the moment before.

Ten dollars, she said to Preach, Queen!'s delight.

Fhill emerged from an aisle with the mechanical bank in hand.

How much for this?

Mrs. Overness hesitated. O, I don't know. Who can put a price tag on history—

Preach, Queen! sucked his teeth. The dealers and collectors—
True, Mrs. Overness said.
She recalled the bullish customers who thought their bank accounts more important than her purpose.
After a moment she said to Fhill,
Just take it.

And that's how Jolly Nigger Bank went home with Fhill.
Installed on a shelf in her kitchen just beneath the spice rack.
Perched there, in an orbit of its own.
As Earth circumnavigated Sun and the distance a beam of light traveled in a single planetary year

Then.
One day.
Fhill noticed.
There was a yellowed postcard in the kitchen drawer.
It bore an image of a grinning black boy eating a watermelon slice bigger than he was.
And just as mysteriously there appeared this magnet on the refrigerator door.
A day or so later she was flabbergasted by the sight of the knotty-headed rag doll sitting on the floor in her living room

What the hell! Fhill screamed the next morning.
When, to her surprise, there sat Aunt Jemima and Uncle Moses, the salt and pepper shakers, those brightly colored visions of service, in her bathtub.
She was baffled.
Where had these things come from?
Why were they in her house?
Why were they multiplying?
Was someone or something playing a trick on her?
Was she having an out-of-body experience?
The whole situation was just too mysterious.
If anybody could get to the bottom of all this, that flame, Theme Le Roy, could.
Theme could carry her into a different reality.

With just a touch.

And the time it took pleasure.

But when the private detective's phone went to voicemail, Fhill hung up without leaving a message.

Though the hunger was still there, so was the left without goodbye.

O well, she tended herself.

That was then, this is now

And though she did not see it move, Jolly Nigger Bank now sat atop her refrigerator.

Grinning, as Fhill left the house and knocked on the Nigerian Woman's door.

Aguta could immediately see something was wrong.

So, he made a pot of lemon balm and poured his sister a mug full of the tea.

Its sweet lemon scent wafted from the cup under her nose.

Fhill sat on the couch, the Nigerian Woman beside her.

He arranged the fish tail of his spaghetti-strapped pink evening gown.

What is it my sister? Tell me, Aguta coaxed Fhill.

And with that, Fhill cried into her tea tearful paragraphs of monsters who'd invaded her house, and Theme, and the ridiculous expectations of a good fuck.

I see, the Nigerian Woman nodded when Fhill finally took a breath.

Aguta found Fhill's story confusing.

But she'd once heard Chinua Achebe theorize, "There is no story that is not true."

Though Fhill's story was not an impossible narrative, it was, certainly, not an incredible one.

As evening wore on, the Nigerian Woman wondered when the tea's calming properties might take hold.

And when they ultimately did, Fhill lapsed into a deep, rhythmic snore.

Unaware of the doorbell ringing.

Or the man who came to visit Aguta bearing pink peonies

The next day, Fhill's house felt slightly off balance.

The cleaned kitchen looked dirty.

The living room floor, unexplainably greasy.

The bathroom bore a nonhuman smell.

And though Fhill was truly disturbed by these events, she was also under a spell

A few nights later, Fhill stopped in at The Fabulous.

For some company.

The crowd was small but the faces familiar.

A few nodded in casual embrace before returning to conversation, staring into the dimmed light.

Fhill spotted Preach, Queen!

The professor sat next to a balding, dark-complected gentleman in a gray shark-skin suit.

The man listened with an intimate intensity as Preach, Queen! read to him.

Fhill marched over to them.

Hey, she greeted the two men.

Hey baby, Preach, Queen! said. You remember Etienne?

Of course, Fhill said. Though she hadn't seen him around lately

Etienne Cadet was accustomed to a quieter life.

As one of the campus librarians, he was in love with books.

He spent most of his awake and asleep time with them.

Until the day he'd met the exuberant Professor Nugent Baldwin Beam.

Who'd, simply put, aroused him.

And he'd cupped, instinctively with his hands, the evidence behind his zipper.

Come by our bar, the professor had crooned. Let me introduce you to my Preach, Queen!

Fhill extended a hand. *Bonswa.*

Bonswa, Etienne gave her hand a firm shake.

As always, he smelled of vetiver bottomed by vanilla.

How pleasant to see you, he said.

Sit down girl, Preach, Queen! commanded. I was just reading from *Blackness and Vernaculars of the Possible.* You know, reading is foreplay.

Never thought of it that way, Fhill sat on the stool next to him.

The professor has no boundaries, Etienne laughed.

He signaled to Overness.

The bartender came with a bottle and a glass immediately.

He poured Fhill a shot of rum then refills for the other two.

Preach, Queen! scrutinized Fhill. Gurl. You. Look tired.

Fhill downed her shot and Preach, Queen!'s too.

I think I'm seeing things. Her eyes scanned the bar's patrons.

She looked paranoid and fearful.

They're watching me, Fhill said.

What? Etienne looked around.

People were involved in conversation and desire.

I don't think so, he said.

I know what I'm seeing, Fhill insisted.

Seeing or being shown? Preach, Queen! said.

In my house, Fhill said. That's right. In my house.

And then, while swilling shots of the dark, tasty rum, she told the lovers a story of caricatures born on plantations

Monstrous Intimacies, Etienne said, confident, when Fhill was finished.

He'd read Christina Sharpe's book several times.

Taken pages of notes inscribed in his journal's memory.

As a book was sacred, and it was his practice never to desecrate one.

With his eyes closed, Etienne recited, "Monstrous intimacies, the everyday mundane horrors" of violation, violence, and intimate forms of domination "that aren't acknowledged to be horrors."[23]

A postcard, a salt and pepper shaker, a bank, toy, all manner of whatnot.

"'That are breathed in like air and often unacknowledged to be monstrous."[24]

Yes! Preach, Queen! exclaimed. Christina Sharpe.

Who? Fhill said.

Preach, Queen! turned to Etienne, I love it when you talk dirty like that.

You're just sapiosexual, Etienne blushed.

Y'all freaking me out, Fhill said.

She felt the rum in her blood now.

Time for me to go home.

---

23 Christina Sharpe, *Monstrous Intimacies: Making Post-Slavery Subjects* (Durham: Duke University Press, 2010), 3.

24 Ibid.

And do your homework, Preach, Queen! instructed.

Homework?

Home. Work. Preach, Queen! punctuated each syllable. Who your ancestors are—

When Fhill left the bar, she was a bit tipsy and thoroughly frustrated.

She'd found the conversation with Preach, Queen! and his lover more confusing than it'd been helpful.

It was the couple talk, she concluded at her front door.

Couples had their own, clingy language.

It was annoying

No sooner did she open her door and walk in, did she hear a voice.

It emanated from the kitchen.

As she came face to face with it, Jolly Nigger Bank—perched atop the kitchen table, accompanied by Watermelon Boy, White Baby's Doll, and Mammy Salt and Pappy Pepper—grinned.

Fhill's eyes popped in fright as she took the scene in.

Feed me, the bank said.

What? Fhill hollered, unsure of what was happening.

Her heart palpitated.

She felt afraid.

Feed me, the bank persisted.

Jesus the devil, Fhill screamed, what world is this?

I eat dreams, Jolly Nigger Bank droned. I eat dreams.

And it locked her eyes with its own

Well, Fhill just stood where she was.

She couldn't move.

Oddly enough, she felt relaxed and heavy at the same time.

She could hear, but she had no desire to speak.

And now, hypnotized, she instantly felt the urge to go to bed.

And sleep.

And so, under the bank's spell night after night, Fhill dreamed.

And when morning came, she recalled her dreams for Jolly Nigger Bank.

Dutifully

So it was.

With each passing day. Fhill lived less and less in our world.

She stayed at home.

She lost her appetite.

She lost weight.

Unwashed and unkempt, she refused to answer her door one evening when Aguta knocked with his worry.

Fhill howled in a tongue she thought was, but was surely more than, human.

When the Nigerian Woman put his ear to her door, he heard only Fhill talking.

What was happening in there?

Why had she locked herself away?

Had she gone mad?

Had she?

Though he couldn't bear the not knowing, the Nigerian Woman returned to his own house.

Saddened

Aguta brewed a pot of tea.

What if she is mad? he told himself.

Was madness a bad thing?

Or something more than an alternate reality?

Why were alternate realities—the ecosystems of dreams, visions, thirst, hungers of the flesh, the ecstatic *hah* at the end of the galaxy's every sentence, its every breath—so misunderstood?

The Nigerian Woman longed to see his sister.

To help her with her troubles.

To be with her in a reality they shared.

But he was willing to wait, and so he consoled himself.

These were difficult times.

Every news story said so.

His sister had a right to refuse.

She had a right to escape.

To live in a different possibility, an otherwhere, if and when she chose to.

And though neither Aguta nor Fhill knew, at that moment, in that otherwhere,

Fhill had entered a state of phistcrate[25]

Then, one night.
One night when Fhill crawled into bed.
Weak from lack of nourishment.
Her skin a sour black.
Her lips dry and cracked.
Her body had had enough of the spell, but.
As it was every night now, she went to sleep dutifully.
She dreamed:
She was in an ocean.
Not on a boat or swimming.
Walking.
On the ocean floor

She came upon a group of people-beings.
She understood the line of them as related
to her, one of them said.
We FromAgo.
Divers and swimmers and sailors and fishers.
A little one said, Simbi.
Then the little one said, We weave
amphibious lives.
And all at once, she began
to thrash about her arms and legs.
Beat against the water.
O,
I am drowning, she cried.
After that, she saw the words,

---

25 Phistcrate [fee cate] becoming and living as a triangle; in a simultaneity of beingness that
     creates or is creative of a shift to come in the praxis of one's spirit, wherein one is the spoken,
     the unspoken, the unspeakable all at once, i.e., the historical black she—those individuals
     who, across what are known as genders and beyond normative constrictions of desire and
     blackness, bent or separated from time what was "black" and "female" in the so-called "new
     world;" vernacular for "whose feet carry my feet, whose breath I breathe." Word created by
     Alexis De Veaux, www.livingdictionaryproject.com/inventedwords

We know.

Get up.

Drink a glass of water

And Fhill awoke immediately.

She made her way, half asleep, in the dark.

The kitchen's tap water cooled the fever sleep.

As she returned to her bedroom

The next morning.

When Fhill opened her eyes.

Jolly Nigger Bank sat in her bed.

Fhill bolted up in alarm.

What the fuck! She shook involuntarily.

Frightened by the monster's nearness.

What do you *want* from me? she yelled. *What?*

Jolly Nigger Bank was nonchalant. Feed me, it calmly stated.

Okay, okay, Fhill bargained. Just give it what it wants, she told herself.

I dreamt about my people.

I think they were my people.

They said they were FromAgo.

O really, Jolly Nigger Bank raised an invisible eyebrow.

Yeah, Fhill said. FromAgo.

And then, as she began to relay the details of her dream, Jolly Nigger Bank became visibly agitated.

Stop! It screamed when it could hear no more. Stop!

This is a nightmare—

It was a dream, Fhill protested.

But Jolly Nigger Bank leapt from her bed.

It ran about her bedroom helter-skelter.

As its agitation grew, it grew more erratic.

It bumped into furniture.

Its roll-up-in-the-head big eyes seemingly blinded.

Then Jolly Nigger Bank ran from the bedroom.

It ran through her house.

Looked crazy.

Fhill followed and watched it, terrified.
The bruising red lecherous mouth spoke in a loud, garbled tongue it thought
was, but was not, human.
It screamed, Watermelon! Doll Baby! Ole Mammy! Ole Pappy!
Squealing from the corners of Fhill's rooms, its companions rushed to its side.
As Jolly Nigger Bank led them to the open kitchen window.
And, holding hands, they all jumped to the street.
Right before they got to the corner of her block, Fhill watched as the band of
monsters vanished

Fhill blinked at the spot where they'd disappeared.
After a while, she breathed deeply.
For the first time in a long time.
She felt released.
The portal in the water had opened.
The monster could not live in water that dreams

Fhill turned her attention to the kitchen, for she had become instantly famished.
But she felt an overwhelming urge to drive down to the coast.
As her silver blue Cadillac convertible swam the highway toward its destination,
she heard the call.
Get in the water.
Be embraced by the underneath.
Breathe there

PRAISE YOU

All who have crossed over in my family, all the ancestors unknown and known to me:
Ruby Moore Hill, daughter of William Moore and Mollie White Moore
Richard Hill, father of me. William Hill, uncle to me
Grand Daddie, father of Mae De Veaux, my mother

Praise you, Valerie Maynard
Breath and Will and Love and Resistance
Praise you, Courage and Every Flaw

Praise The Beloved:

Sokari Ekine and Woza Beanz our Nommo Canine and adrienne maree brown the wondrous and Shayde Mary Beth and Zamir Boger and Kathy Engel and Amy Horowitz and Fred Hudson and Briona S. Jones and Marilyn Doucette and Averil Lazard and Nalo Zidan and Mark Anthony Neal and Cheryl Clarke and Carole Byard and Keguro Macharia and Ella Engel Snow and Antonio David Lyons and Steven G. Fullwood and Alexis Pauline Gumbs and Sangodare Akinwale and Carl Sagan and Cheryl Clarke and Ola Osaze and Brenna Clarke and Jenna Wortham and Justine Alexis Engel Snow and Tei Okamoto and Junauda Petrus-Nasah and The Elderberries and Ngowo Nasah and Amy Nesbitt and Nana Fofie Amina Bashir and praise this planet and Christopher Stahling and Deborah and Odell De Veaux and E. Patrick Johnson and Kristina Kay Robinson and Gwendolen Hardwick and Kerry James Marshall and Rachel Zaslow and Fahima Ife and Priscilla Hale and Erin Sharkey and Zoe Hollomon and Jon Snow and Sharon Bridgforth and Dena Fisher and Ericka Jones-Craven and Cindee and Nathaniel De Veaux and Adam Evans and The Enclave Habitat and Geo Smith and Omi Jones and Eric Darnell Pritchard and David Sanchez and Yesenia Montilla and Erna Sensiba and Matice Moore and Marie Dutton Brown and Nina Simone and the amphibious black diaspora and the black that is New Orleans and what we call the good black queer life

And for teaching me other realms, praise you:

Elizabeth Alexander, *The Black Interior: Essays* (2004); David Pilgrim, *Understanding Jim Crow, Using Racist Memorabilia to Teach Tolerance and Promote Social Justice* (2015); Toni Morrison, *The Black Book* (1974); Barbara Christian, "The Race for Theory" (1988); Omise'eke Natasha Tinsley, *Ezili's Mirrors, Imagining Black Queer Genders* (2018); Audre Lorde in Alexis De Veaux, *Warrior Poet, A Biography of Audre Lorde* (2004); Judith Gleason, *Oya, In Praise of the Goddess* (1987); Emilie M. Townes, ed., *A Troubling in My Soul: Womanist Perspectives on Evil and Suffering* (1993); William R. Jones, "Theodicy and Racism" (1973); Jayna Brown, *Black Utopias, Speculative Life and the Music of Other Worlds* (2021); Ashon T. Crawley, *Black Pentecostal Breath, The Aesthetics of Possibility* (2017); Victoria Glendinning, "Lies and Silences" (1988); Andreas Weber, *Matter and Desire, An Erotic Ecology* (2014); Betty Deramus, *Forbidden Fruit, Love Stories from The Underground Railroad* (2005); E. Patrick Johnson, ed., *No Teas, No Shade, New Writings in Black Queer Studies* (2016): Ella Engel Snow, livingdictionaryproject.com; Katherine McKittrick, *Demonic Grounds, Black Women and the Cartographies of Struggle* (2006); West African Wisdom, Adinkra symbols and Meanings; Sandra Jackson and Julie E. Moody-Freeman, *The Black Imagination, Science Fiction, Futurism and the Speculative* (2011); D. Scott Miller, "*The AfroSurreal Manifesto: Black Is the New Black—A Twenty-First Century Manifesto* (2009); Robin Devoe, *Dictionary of the Strange, Curious, and the Lovely* (2017); Lynell L. Thomas, *Desire and Disaster in New Orleans: Tourism, Race, and Historical Memory* (2014); Christina Sharpe, *Monstrous Intimacies, Making Post-Slavery Subjects* (2010); Chinua Achebe, *Things Fall Apart* (1958); Carl Zimmer, *Life's Edge: The Search for What It Means to be Alive* (2021); Raphael Chijoke Njoku, *West African Masking Traditions and Diaspora Masquerade Carnivals, History, Memory, and Transnationalism* (2020); Kimberly Drew and Jenna Wortham, eds., *Black Futures* (2020); Shirlette Ammons, *Matching Skin* (2008); Shantrelle P. Lewis, *Dandy Lion, The Black Dandy and Street Style* (2017); and La Marr Jurelle Bruce, *How to Go Mad Without Losing Your Mind: Madness and Black Radical Creativity* (2021).

The following parables appeared, in slightly different versions, in these publications:

"Girl Negro," *NOW: An Online Journal* (Hobart Festival of Women Writers), no. 1 (2020): www.hfwwnow.com.

"City of Parables," *NOW: An Online Journal* (Hobart Festival of Women Writers), no. 2 (2021): www.hfwwnow.com.

"Inter**species**," *Mouths of Rain: An Anthology of Black Lesbian Thought*, ed. Briona Simone Jones (New York: The New Press, 2021).

"The Wake," *The Naked Chef, Series 1*, text by Alexis De Veaux, photos by Sokari Ekine (New Orleans, 2020)

"The Wake: A Parable," *Feminist Studies* 48, no. 1 (2022).